The
13
Culprits

(Les 13 Coupables)

Georges Simenon on the *Ostrogoth*, 1929
Where He Wrote *Les 13 Coupables*

Georges Simenon

The 13 Culprits

(Les 13 Coupables)

FIRST ENGLISH TRANSLATION BY PETER SCHULMAN

Crippen & Landru Publishers
Norfolk, Virginia
2002

Cover by Deborah Miller

Crippen & Landru logo by Eric D. Greene

ISBN (limited edition): 1-885941-78-1

ISBN (trade edition): 1-885941-79-X

FIRST EDITION

10 9 8 7 6 5 4 3 2 1

Printed in the United States of America on acid-free, recycled paper

Crippen & Landru, Publishers
P. O. Box 9315
Norfolk, VA 23505
USA

E-Mail: CrippenL@Pilot.Infi.Net
Web: www.crippenlandru.com

CONTENTS

INTRODUCTION

"I haven't written that much. I'm already 29 and I've only published 277 books ..." a brash, young Georges Simenon explained to a famous journalist at the time. "It's not my profession," he explained. "By profession, I'm a traveler, or an explorer, if you will. I come in from the Baltic, and a month later I'm off again, maybe for Oceania."[1] When Simenon was commissioned in 1929 to write his series of short stories — *The 13 Mysteries, The 13 Enigmas* and *The 13 Culprits* — for *Détective*, a magazine published by Gallimard under the editorship of his two friends, Joseph and Georges Kessel, he was traveling up and down the canals and ports of Europe in a cutter he had just had built for himself, *The Ostrogoth*. Simenon had even had it baptized by the abbot of Notre-Dame cathedral in Paris when it was moored at the Pont-Neuf. High on the money coming in from his successful crime and pulp novels, Simenon took to the seas with "Tigy" (his wife Régine's nickname), "Boule" (his nickname for Henriette Liberge, a seventeen-year-old farm girl who became his loyal servant and mistress) and his Great Dane, Olaf. Tired of the sleepy, industrial towns of his childhood in Belgium, Simenon craved the freedom of the open seas where, with his typewriter on a folding table, and his backside on a folding chair, he could simultaneously lock himself up, write prolifically and travel to any destination he pleased.

It was on the *Ostrogoth* that Simenon wrote *The 13 Culprits*, the

---

[1] Quoted by Pierre Assouline in *Simenon: A Biography*. New York: Alfred A. Knopf, 1997, p. 105.

third series of mystery stories for *Détective* magazine which were designed to be stopped a few paragraphs before the ending so that readers could guess at the solutions. The first series, *The 13 Mysteries*, brought in so much mail to the magazine, according to Simenon, "that mailmen had to haul it in by the sackful, and more than forty people had to be hired to check the answers."[2] When his publishers asked him to write a series that was harder to figure out, he wrote *The 13 Enigmas*. The "answers" to the stories in *The 13 Culprits*, the last series, were meant to be the most difficult to guess. Each story appeared in two parts, the mystery in one issue and the solution in a later one in order to insure that the reading experience felt like a magazine game. They were originally published under one of Simenon's pseudonyms, Georges Sim, but when they were collected in book form in 1932, they were among the first works published under the name "Georges Simenon." Prior to these ludic short stories, Simenon read many works of modern criminology in order to get into the detective's thought process. While he was dutifully studying this methodology, he also published, under another pseudonym, J.K. Charles, a series of short, slightly fictionalized reports of police methods in a weekly magazine titled *Ric et Rac.*[3]

An interesting adventure, worthy of a thriller, took place on the *Ostrogoth* during the writing of the "13" series. Stopping in

---

[2] Quoted by Simenon in his *Intimate Memoirs*. San Diego, New York, London: Harcourt Brace Jovanovich, 1984, p. 26.

[3] See Stanley G. Eskin's excellent *Simenon: A Critical Biography*. Jefferson, North Carolina and London: McFarland & Company, 1987, p.76.

Introduction

Wilhelmshaven, a German port in Lower Saxony (which readers of *The 13 Culprits* will recognize as being the birthplace of Otto Müller), Simenon's ship, which was brandishing a French flag, instantly drew the suspicions of the local authorities as Wilhelmshaven was also a repository for rusting, dry-docked World War I submarines. As Pierre Assouline has described it, Simenon, who was oblivious to politics at that time, found himself in a tense political situation without knowing it: "The economic crisis had just broken out, and the country was governed by a coalition led by a Social Democratic chancellor. The leader of the National People's Party had recently formed an alliance with Adolf Hitler. Within a few months the fall of the Müller government would seal the fate of the parliamentary republic."[4] Within moments of his mooring, the police helped him get supplies which they even carried on board his ship as though they were porters. Later, a plainclothes counterespionage agent came aboard and questioned him for two hours. After searching the ship thoroughly, the agent "discovered a typewriter and an easel, tried to decipher one of Simenon's novels as though cracking a secret code,"[5] before bringing him to Police Headquarters. As Simenon has recounted in his *Intimate Memoirs*, the German police officers were particularly alarmed by his correspondence with his editors at *Détective* :

> "Why did you come in to Wilhelmshaven? Since the end of the war not a single French boat has put in here."
> I kept trying to make sense out of the questions he threw at me,

---

[4] Assouline, p. 85.

[5] Assouline, p. 85.

often unexpectedly, since he kept craftily switching the subject.
"And how does it happen that you receive telegrams that are signed 'Detective'?"
This one spoke French well, in spite of his accent. He had probably been part of the occupation forces.
"Are you a detective?"
"No. That's a weekly that publishes crime stories."
"Then, are you a policeman?"
"No, but I write stories about detectives."
"Why?"
"Because I get orders for them."
"In other words, you are carrying out orders?"

Although Simenon was nervous, and sweating profusely in fear of being arrested, he was summarily ordered by the Polizeipräsidium to sign a deposition and leave the country at once.

✢ ✢ ✢

As Stanley G. Eskin has observed, although the "13" series was published a year before the birth of Maigret, who would make his first appearance in the 1930 novel *Pietr-le-Letton*, they were written in "a mode quite contrary to the Maigret spirit, as if he were zigzagging toward Maigret and this were a last zag in the opposite direction."[6] As Eskin understands it, the detectives featured in the series, Leborgne, G.7, and Froget, are "anti-Maigrets in being wholly, and frivolously, intellectual, in contrast with the intuitive Maigret, who keeps saying,

---

[6] Eskin, p. 76.

Introduction

'I never think.' "[7] Yet, as one can see in *The 13 Culprits*, Froget, the formidable Examining Magistrate, is a master in criminology and psychology. With "the whiteness of his skin, of his old fashioned Bressant hair style, and of his starched linen" (as he is described in the opening sentences of "Ziliouk," p. 19), Froget is an imposing character who is not only in rigid control of his own emotions, but also of the poor suspects who come before him and whom he is able to manipulate psychologically as though they were puppets. As the narrator explains, Froget is so effective because he lets the thirteen culprits disintegrate on their own in court: "Most Examining Magistrates accumulate series of questions, endeavor to confuse the accused from whom they often extract the sort of sentence which can pass for a confession. Monsieur Froget, on the other hand, gave his opponent time to think *and even time to think too much*" (p. 25). In *The 13 Culprits*, it is always the guilty ones who are ultimately responsible for setting up their own nooses.

It is this rather icy, yet old fashioned aspect of Froget's character that we endeavored to convey in this translation at Crippen & Landru — the first translation into English, in fact, of *The 13 Culprits* in its entirety. Earlier, between 1942 and 1948, the famed critic and editor Anthony Boucher had translated a few of the stories for *Ellery Queen's Mystery Magazine* (as well as some stories from *The 13 Enigmas* and *The 13 Mysteries*) but never the entire collection which has been mysteriously overlooked until now. Contrary to Boucher's translations which were very creative, but sometimes took liberties with Simenon's writing, I have stuck quite loyally to the text, and tried to preserve Simenon's elegant, sometimes labyrinthine, formal sentence

---

[7] Ibid.

structures which, I feel, are not only reflective of Froget's thinking, and even of his personality, but also convey a period, the 1920's, and an atmosphere of propriety that is no longer as present in the Paris of today.

As such, I have tried to maintain the flavor of Simenon's Paris at the time, a different Paris from the playground described by Hemingway, for example, in *A Movable Feast*, or the familiar image of the carefree universe evoked by Josephine Baker (with whom Simenon had been romantically involved). Rather it is a marginal Paris, populated by what the French would label *des ratés*, society's losers who, for one reason or another, are brought down by a petty vice, or a greedy aspiration, that invariably leads to a bitter sense of failure in their lives ... and, of course, a crime they hubristically think they can get away with. It is the lonely city within all levels of the Parisian mosaic; a Paris made up of eccentric individuals who all, in some manner or another, feel as though they have been hung out to dry on the fringes of society: Monsieur Rodrigues, "an old male coquette", whose seedy, decadent apartment on the rue Bonaparte is also somehow a reflection of his scheming, vengeful persona; on the southern tip of Paris, by the Porte d'Orléans metro station, Madame Smitt's decrepit boarding house attempts to shelter her past and her fortune, along with the misfits who are temporarily housed there; the exotic Nouchi whose "painfully sought out elegance" reveals her irresistible urge to penetrate the generous Mrs. Crosby's fancy apartment on the rue François-1er; the enigmatic Waldemar Strvzeski, eaten up by a biting regret at not having advanced in the Polish military, but who is relegated instead to the peripheries of the Polish criminal gangs hanging out at the sleazy Saint-Antoine Bar in the primarily working class sections of northern Paris; the fetishistic Enesco, nicknamed "The Pacha" by the prostitutes he enjoys burning within the confines of his luxurious suite in the Grand Hotel ... Often coming from either romantic but murky locations such as "the Orient," Eastern Europe, the Netherlands or Harlem, Simenon's characters never fit in to the respective societies from which they crave acceptance. The spaces that the culprits create for themselves (or are condemned to) are often indicative of the inner turmoil that eventually dooms them, such as Philippe's claustrophobic "strange lodging on the rue Bréa" with windows that had never been washed and "old carpets everywhere, pieces of discolored material, spread out along the walls"; the transient world of the failed circus performers, the Timmermans, who must live from one third rate hotel to another; or the especially depressing "Flemings" living as a sort of "Commune" on the outskirts of Paris in an isolated and miserable shanty in the middle of some fields ...

Above all, Simenon captures the painful isolation and loneliness of these characters who despite occasionally maintaining pretenses of grandeur or outlandish ambitions are all in some way uncomfortable with themselves. Simenon's Paris is indeed the same Paris he enjoyed wandering through as a young man, the Paris of street walkers, pimps and thieves that he often sought out to calm "a corner of his soul [which] was never still."[8] As Fenton Bresler has described it, it is this world that Simenon felt inexorably drawn to when the rest of Paris was tucked into their beds: "He used to spend nights wandering, unarmed, on the old defence works that still existed near La Villette [...] He claims proudly that the infamous neighborhood of the Canal St. Martin held no secrets for him, nor did the alleys of Montmartre

---

[8] As portrayed by Fenton Bresler in *The Mystery of Georges Simenon: A Biography*. Toronto, Ontario: General Publishing Co, 1983, p.55.

nor the narrow byways of the 12th Arrondissement. He made love in the streets and in the passageways, 'where the unexpected arrival of a policeman could have changed my future.' "[9] Searching for prostitutes, while his wife was safe at home, Simenon reveled in nocturnal transgressions and digressions which no doubt found their way into the sins of his shady, displaced and forever ungratified characters ...

Another stylistic device that I have maintained in this translation is Simenon's potentially confusing switching of tenses. Indeed, he often jostles the present, the past, and the future within a paragraph, or even a sentence. This was a conscious decision on Simenon's part in order to create a cinematic effect, and a suspenseful feeling of immediacy. As he explains it: "To my thinking, in my philosophy, past, present and future do not exist ... It's as though everything happens at the same time. Because everything depends on what we have experienced before and prepares us for what we are going to experience."[10] As Simenon wrote to André Gide, the "dean of letters" at that time, regarding a short story he had written in 1925, the issue of the tenses was almost a metaphysical one for him: "I was already haunted by a problem that has pursued me ever since: the three dimensions — the past, the present and the future — tying themselves together in a single action with a density of atmosphere and of complete verisimilitude."[11]

Related to the fluidity of tenses is Simenon's frequent use of ellipses (...) as punctuation. Their indefiniteness, their hinting at things not

---

[9] Bresler, p. 55.

[10] Quoted by Bresler, p. 53.

[11] Quoted by Bresler, p. 54.

Introduction

quite said, is important in Simenon's style, and I have retained them in almost all instances.

In 2002, Simenon's Paris may seem like a thing of the past, a museum-ification perhaps of an element of society that had fallen through the cracks of history, or even of everyday life, but whose slippery existence did not escape the night watch of Simenon's tourism through the at times invisible underbelly of the Parisian landscape. It is this Paris that the thirteen culprits haunt, a Paris captured by Simenon in 1929, at the time the great Depression had brought down the frolicking gaiety of America's "roaring twenties." Perhaps the discovery of these short stories today will allow them to continue to haunt the dark Parisian streets and boulevards through this translation, which, like the many other works that the prolific Simenon produced, will further corroborate why both Dashiell Hammett and Raymond Chandler considered him to be their favorite mystery writer.

Peter Schulman
Old Dominion University
Norfolk, VA
June 5, 2002

The First Culprit

ZILIOUK

ZILIOUK

THE OPPONENTS were evenly matched. In fact, the general word in the public prosecutor's office was that Monsieur Froget, the Examining Magistrate,[1] would finally fall on his face, which would not be entirely displeasing to every one.

He sat in front of his desk in a seemingly uncomfortable position. One of his shoulders was higher than the other, his head hunched forward. As usual, he was all black and white — the whiteness of his skin, of his old fashioned Bressant hair style, and of his starched linen; the blackness of his formal three-piece suit. He was, in short, slightly anachronistic. There had been many a time when others had wondered whether age had finally crept up on him, as there was a certain aspect to him that made him look sixty years old.

I had been a frequent visitor to his house on the Champ-de-Mars and I would like to offer my personal impressions of him. No man had ever been able to crush me, or had me doubt my own opinion of myself as much as Monsieur Froget. I would tell him a story, for example. He would look at me in a way that might appear slightly encouraging. I would finish. I would wait for an opinion, a comment, a smile. He would always stare at me fixedly as though he were focusing on a landscape or a piece of evidence, then he would finally let out a little sigh. Well, I swear to you, there's such an intensity in a moment like that it would give one enough humility to last a

---

[1] *Juge d'Instruction*, a position combining judicial and police functions. He is often addressed as *"monsieur le juge."*

lifetime. Nothing but a sigh! A breath of air! This is how I would interpret his response: "And you went through so much trouble just to tell me that?"

This was an example, by the way, of only the most superficial aspect of his personality and I will no doubt get a chance to speak about what I might have gleaned about his true nature.

Nonetheless, that day in his office, a struggle was taking place in the manner that I have just described that one could not even qualify as icy. He was dealing with Ziliouk, that world-renowned adventurer who had been in all the papers for weeks, a Hungarian (or Polish, or Lithuanian, or Latvian, nobody knew exactly) Jew who, at twenty-five, had already been expelled from five or six countries in Europe.

He had been arrested in his luxurious Paris residence (was he now thirty-five years old — or forty — or thirty — or less — or more?) after a warrant issued by the President of the Council to whom he had proposed a business arrangement in his usual commodity: diplomatic documents.

Genuine or fraudulent? General opinion was split. Ziliouk had already sold Soviet documents to England which had caused a ministerial crisis and a breaking off of diplomatic relations between the two countries. He had sold Japanese papers to America and American ones to the Japanese. There were signs of his activities in Bulgaria, in Serbia, in Rome and in Madrid.

He was quite handsome. He was more than elegant: he was almost opulent, and yet he sported, on the whole, a heavy *flashy* foreign accent.

Monarchs, Heads of State had all written to him. He had infiltrated most of the world's diplomatic circles.

As soon as he was arrested, he had become aggressive. "Eventually you will be forced to release me, and then you'll be in hot water!"

He would insinuate that he was in fact working for the *Deuxième Bureau*[2] (against and on behalf of everyone) and that he had close ties to the British Secret Service.

Not one single magistrate had wanted anything to do with this case. It was the kind of case that would break the back of an honest Examining Magistrate and put a sad end to his career.

There was Ziliouk, dressed in his three-piece suit from the best tailor in London, immaculate, with a vague smile on his face. An hour had gone by and Monsieur Froget still would not speak to him. With the minute and precise gestures of a mouse nibbling at food, he read the mobile squad's report, at the top of which the accused could make out, in upside down letters: *The Ziliouk Affair*.

He read through them seemingly for the first time. Then he would look at the accused with that stare that was all his own, that concentrated stare that was as heavy as lead. It could not be compared to what can be called a piercing look, nor was it prophetic. It wasn't ferocious either. It was a calm gaze, that would slowly zero-in on a target and remain locked on it for hours and hours from that moment on.

Ziliouk's first words were, as he lit a fancy cigarette with a calculated flippancy: "Smoke slightly bothers me ..." And, perhaps for the first time in his career, the adventurer felt ill at ease. Out of a need for bravado, he felt he had to declare: "I would prefer to warn you that your efforts will be in vain! I have been accused of selling false documents to France. I defy you to put me away on that charge. I have also been accused of providing Germany with equally counterfeit

---

[2]An elite, French counter-intelligence unit similar to Britain's MI5.

diplomatic documents in respect to French foreign policy ... Nobody has seen these documents! The only accuser is an underling working for the *Deuxième Bureau* and I'll do my best to prove that he's playing both sides, just as I'll do my best to prove that I was extremely useful to the *Deuxième Bureau* ..."

There was no reply. Monsieur Froget lowered his eyes onto a new report which he read in its entirety. This went on for an hour! And Ziliouk searched in vain for any sign of curiosity, of fever, of passion, in short: any trace of human emotion. He spoke once again. "Even if I am found guilty, I'll get three years maximum, just as X ... and Z ... (he named spies who had recently been convicted by the French courts). After that, France will have to pay dearly!"

The papers crackled before Monsieur Froget. The judge continued to read. He had Ziliouk's identity papers in front of him, each one more counterfeit than the next. In truth, one would have a hard time establishing for certain that he was born in one country rather than another. In turn, he had called himself Carlyle, Sunbeam, Smit, Keller, Lipton, Rochet. There had undoubtedly been other names as well ...

He had been carrying fifty thousand dollars in his pocket at the time of his arrest!

Monsieur Froget had not yet asked a single question after an hour and a half of this *tête-à-tête*. The report he had just read was a military one. Ten years earlier, Ziliouk had been arrested in Germany under somewhat mysterious circumstances. He had been released a month later, even more mysteriously, and had, in the meantime, been visited in his cell by one of the chiefs of the Wilhelmstrasse.[3]

That this man was dangerous ... that was obvious! That he was

---

[3]Offices of the German government.

riffraff, he bragged about it! But as he said himself, he left no loophole for action in the courts.

And Monsieur Froget remained motionless, his left shoulder still higher than his right one, his indifferent gaze landing at times on his papers, or at other times on the accused. "Do you recognize this photograph of your last mistress?" he asked in a cheerless manner.

Ziliouk burst out laughing. "Barely, *monsieur le juge!* Barely! She was a charming girl from Picratt's, the bar on the rue Daunou ... I rarely saw her ..."

And his laughter became ambiguous, smutty almost. He dared to add: "Is she a friend of yours?"

"What language did you use to speak with her?"

Once again, Ziliouk felt like being vulgar. He answered with a sentence that is impossible to print but which did not make the magistrate flinch in the least.

"Well then, at certain times, she spoke to you in a *patois* from Lille, and you answered her in this same dialect, which bothered her, because she did not think that she was understood by a foreigner; she had said certain things which were rather derogatory."

Ziliouk remained silent. The judge remained silent for almost a quarter of an hour. The file was examined, slowly, followed by a file which bore in big letters on its yellow envelope: *The Stephen Affair.*

Ziliouk was able to read the thick letters, just as Monsieur Froget could. And the former allocated enough time to prepare his answers, his every attitude.

It was an eight-year old file that had been classified for as many years. It pertained to a certain woman named Stephen, who had been married to Pierre Stephen, and who had been murdered under rather troubling circumstances by her lover, a Polish worker who had disappeared without a trace. Pierre Stephen was a foreman in a chemical factory to which an artillery officer had been detached, presumably for research of considerable interest to national security.

Around that same time, documents — most notably a description of a new gas mask — had disappeared.

At that time, the Stephens were also leading a lifestyle that they were not used to and had made certain expenditures which did not match their actual incomes. And then there was the dramatic event itself: Stephen's wife was found dead at the foot of a coal dump near the factory.

No one knew much of her lover. He had been spotted prowling around the region. He lived in the barracks of a veritable tribe of Polish workers, but his mates did not know what factory he worked for. They did not even know his name. He had disappeared on the very day of the murder.

⁜ ⁜ ⁜

He was sensitive to the fact that the battle was shifting to another level, and from then on Ziliouk's flippancy increased along with his chances of checking into the morgue.

"I do not know what you are trying to insinuate here!" he said with aggressive irony. "If you'd like, I could answer you just as well in a Javanese coolie *patois* or the *argot* of the workers in a Ford plant ..."

This was quite true. He was such a polyglot that one of his files mentions his presence three years earlier in China where he acted as a close advisor to a southern general. At the time of his arrest by an inspector who had been a member of the colonial police, he had noticed a pin on his tie which had been woven by the Moïs of Indo-China and struck up a conversation in the dialect of that tribe.

No words could do justice to Monsieur Froget's disinterest which had not changed since the start of the session. Most Examining Magistrates accumulate series of questions, endeavor to confuse the accused from whom they often extract the sort of sentence which can pass for a confession. Monsieur Froget, on the other hand, gave his opponent time to think *and even time to think too much*. His silences would last several minutes, the questions a few seconds at best. Up till now, he had asked but two. The specialist interested in such matters should count the number of words that issued from Monsieur Froget's lips during the course of this crucial examination.

In a low voice, the judge now read a telegram that he had directed to the public prosecutors' office at Lille.

Question: Where do the Stephens come from? How long had they lived in Lille before the occurrence of that dramatic event?

Answer: From the Loire country. The Stephens arrived in Lille, having come from Saint Etienne, one month before the crime. The Lille Factory requested a few good specialists from the Saint-Etienne branch in order to start production on a new product. Stephen came in with the group that had arrived in the North in June.

Monsieur Froget raised his voice for the third time. "Can you tell me precisely where you were, eight years ago, in the month of June?"

The crime had been committed around mid-July.

"In Berlin!" Ziliouk replied without hesitation. "And if you really want to know, I was in daily contact with the Wihelmstrasse. I have no idea where you are going with this, but I would warn you that you are on the wrong track. I do not know the Stephens."

Monsieur Froget turned the page, read through the last document that the *Deuxième Bureau* had provided him with and said: "Pierre Stephen, foreman at the Saint-Etienne Arms Factory, suspected by his friends of fraternizing with enemy agents, despite any actual proof to that effect, had been sent to Lille (on the recommendation of counter-intelligence) where workers with his expertise were needed around the end of June.

"The purpose was to see whether documents would disappear in this case as well.

"Before it was possible to establish Stephen's guilt, and especially to uncover his accomplices, his wife's murder at the hands of a stranger had changed things and from then onward Stephen's behavior was no longer suspect. Very shaken and prematurely aged by the tragedy, he had left the factory shortly after the dramatic events and became a night watchman for a business in Pantin."

Monsieur Froget had still not even uttered four sentences. He stood up without exhibiting the slightest emotion. He revealed himself to be taller and larger than one would have imagined by just seeing him seated.

He looked at Ziliouk as though at the most everyday object. And he pronounced wearily as though he were a man finishing a chore, as he brushed off his black hat with the inside of his sleeve: "I accuse you of voluntary homicide on the person of the woman Stephen."

✤ ✤ ✤

"Why?" Ziliouk asked, lighting another cigarette.

Monsieur Froget appeared not to have heard him. His attention seemed to be focused on a spot on his hat.

"You have no proof at all!" Ziliouk insisted.

The word "proof" brought Monsieur Froget back to reality. He said slowly: " 'Proof' of your guilt? Here it is: From my file, you could only read the words *The Stephen Affair*. And yet you told me: 'I do not know *the Stephens*.' Your use of the plural is your confession."

Ziliouk absorbed the shock without flinching. He was worthy of his opponent. But he no longer spoke a single word.

Nonetheless, Monsieur Froget did not give much importance to his victory. How could such an easy triumph matter much to him? After glancing once more at his hat, he added, stingily: "A child would have been able to figure this out clearly. Three clues and bits of evidence have convicted you, in addition to your confession, which constitutes the formal evidence against you ..."

Monsieur Froget counted with his fingers: "First of all, your knowledge of the Lille *patois* ... Secondly, the excessive speed and precision with which you answered me when I asked you where you were eight years ago, during the month of June ... Thirdly, the fact that you were a member of German intelligence."

And then he concluded: "An everyday affair. The Stephens provide Ziliouk, a German secret-agent, with documents of interest to national security. When Ziliouk learns that the Stephens are under suspicion and sent to Lille, he fears being turned in by his mistress and being convicted as an accomplice. He decides to eliminate her. After the murder of his wife, who was Ziliouk's tool, the foreman Pierre Stephen's behavior no longer seems suspicious ... Case closed!"

Then Monsieur Froget rang for the guards.

The Second Culprit

Monsieur Rodrigues

MONSIEUR RODRIGUES

THERE WAS only one thing that was bothersome about Monsieur Froget's presence in that apartment perched on the sixth floor of a building on the rue Bonaparte. One could hardly decide what was more shocking, what was even becoming indecent — the apartment or the judge in black, as he focused on the sight of the drinking glasses, which were clear and round like targets.

The two undercover policemen who had brought Monsieur Rodrigues into the apartment remained standing outside the door on the landing. The sheriff had gotten so used to the judge after ten years that his presence fit him like a glove to the point where he even forgot that he was there.

As for Rodrigues himself, he added the final touch to the enigmatic atmosphere; he made it comprehensible, even though a few days of incarceration took the edge off his asperity.

There were five rooms with arched ceilings, as the apartment was directly beneath the line of roofs. There was no sign of any dining room, kitchen, bedroom, and yet the same ambiance permeated the space: a profusion of rugs dominated by purple-tinted reds; trinkets chosen for their strangeness, products emerging from the imaginations of all races, of all eras; couches in all the angles; low tables; pillows strewn about the floor.

The only trace of practicality came from a cracked teapot, empty glasses, uncorked bottles, a Primus brand hot-plate that was left on one of the rugs and a toothbrush that was firmly planted in a champagne glass.

31

There was something both refined and dishonorable about the apartment. It smelled of incense, rare aromas and seediness.

It was in keeping with the master of the house who was tall, thin and who at times resembled a fallen aristocrat and, at other times, a worn-out clown. He was fifty-five years old. He dressed like an adolescent. Moreover, he powdered his face and dyed his hair. If one looked closely, one could make out a thin scar on the tip of his nose. As he would be the first to explain, it resulted from an operation he had undergone in order to change the shape of his nose and to make his face appear more harmonious.

"A man's first duty is to be handsome, just as animals are beautiful, just as flowers are beautiful!" he once told Monsieur Froget.

He was repulsive. An old male coquette. A mixture of senility and a false sense of youth.

The police reports, however, were categorical: His only unusual habit was that his visitors were mostly young people, almost all of them Spanish like him.

Books were scattered everywhere: they were all written by the most opaque of poets.

He was quite at ease, despite the accusation that hung over him. He managed to refrain from showing any fear. As was his custom, his skin was caked with make-up.

He was the first to speak while the judge walked back and forth, as calmly as if he were taking his morning constitutional. "You must admit that you are unable to unearth any evidence whatsoever against me and that had you been handed a thousand clues, you would still have a hard time trying to come up with any plausible explanation for such a crime."

Three psychiatrists confirmed that he was responsible for his actions even though he was quite mad. And yet, he had committed murder! It was a moral and physical certainty, one of those obvious truths which, in some ways, pass for evidence.

Monsieur Rodrigues received many guests. He gave the impression that he was a wealthy man. He enjoyed opium, and young people often came to smoke entire nights at his house, amidst the pillows, the rugs, the drapes, all that silly and somber rubbish that exhaled a pungent aroma made up of drugs, sleeze and human sweat.

At eight o'clock at night, on the previous Tuesday, the *concierge* had seen a young man that she hadn't noticed before go up the stairs. Towards the middle of the night, she heard a strange sound emanating from the staircase. She thought that Monsieur Rodrigues and his guest were drunk, because in the sixth *arrondissement*,[1] people are as addicted to champagne as they are to opium and heroin. She pulled on the door-pull, went to bed, opened the door a little later for a tenant who neglected to mention his name.

"Monsieur Rodrigues would always yell out his name very loudly!" she would remark afterwards to the police.

That morning, a body of a young man was found in the Seine, in front of the rue Bonaparte. He had been thrown from the top of the quay and the body had attached itself quite by chance on a barge's mooring. He had been stabbed three times with a knife. There were no documents found in his pockets. The police were carrying out their investigation. That very day, she identifies the drowned victim: he is the son of the Duke and Duchess of S ... who hold one of the most visible positions in the Spanish royal court.

A detective introduces himself to Monsieur Rodrigues. He has

---

[1] An *arrondissement* is a district of Paris

already established that the victim, who was just passing through Paris, had let himself be dragged along by his rather dubious cohorts on an evening jaunt through Montmartre, Montparnasse and certain bars on the Champs-Elysées. Since S ... wished to become initiated in the ways of opium, they introduced him to Monsieur Rodrigues who had invited him over.

On one of the red carpets, the detective notices a few dark spots which experts consider to be (but without affirming it) human blood stains.

"My goodness! Why not look instead at my finger which I cut on Monday ..." replied Monsieur Rodrigues.

"Did you cut yourself attacking your guest?"

"And why on earth would I have attacked him? I maintain that he left this apartment on his own volition. I had walked him back to the corner of the rue Bonaparte and to the Boulevard Saint-Germain. He was inebriated. He refused to take a taxi as I had suggested. He no doubt retraced his steps, made a wrong move along the quays where some thugs murdered him ..."

"Was this the first time that you had him over?"

"The first. But I had seen him before at the Pickwick's Bar."

"Do you know his name, his family situation?"

"Titles don't impress me!"

And the police report ends with a deposition from a Spaniard who had been at the Pickwick's Bar with S ...and Rodrigues. "S ..., while remaining casual, was nonetheless quite an aristocrat and kept his distances, especially in regards to Rodrigues, whom he considered a bit of a curiosity. He burst out laughing when someone spoke to him about our friend's prestigious but murky roots. I think I remember his crying out at that moment: 'Magnificent! What a unique fellow! ...' "

Monsieur Rodrigues

✛ ✛ ✛

As for Monsieur Froget, he had entered a smaller room which was slightly more decorated than the other ones, and where the window panes distilled a sanctuary-like aura.

A painting appears to dominated the room, grabs one's attention, absorbs all light. The portrait of a woman, in a grand pose, from head to toe. She is young and beautiful, with admirable red hair.

The painter had chosen to portray her completely in the nude.

The canvas is pierced, in the middle, and it had obviously been torn recently.

Monsieur Rodrigues follows the judge's stare as he begins his questioning, the very first question, in fact: "Who is this?"

The accused manages a telling smile, a smile that is at once crooked and reserved, a reflection of his entire persona. The portrait is at least twenty years old.

"Did you receive your guest in this room?"

"In this room, yes!"

And it is on that spot that the traces of blood were found on the Persian carpet!

"On what day did you hurt your finger?"

"Monday. Or rather on the eve of the ..."

"On what day had the painting been torn?"

On that same Monday. It fell. When I tried to put it back up, I hurt myself ..."

"How did you become so wealthy?"

In his wallet, Monsieur Froget holds the answer to a question he had asked via telegraph to the Madrid police. Until he was seventeen, Rodrigues was a simple underling in the Ministry of Foreign Affairs. He suddenly disappears, after having announced to his colleagues and to his superiors that he has just inherited a certain amount of money from his uncle who had settled in South America and that he would be living in Paris from now on. That was where he was tracked down, in fact. Six hundred thousand francs are deposited in his name in a bank on the Avenue de l'Opéra by a notary from Geneva from whom Monsieur Froget possesses a telegram. "No inheritance. Cannot betray professional secret."

Rodrigues, however, does not hesitate to reply:

"I had had some tickets for the end of the year Grand Lottery. You are familiar with our national lottery. One of my numbers was picked.

"The drawing was held at the beginning of January, right?"

"The end of December ..."

"And yet, you left Madrid in September ..."

"I didn't want anyone to know that my fortune came from that lottery."

"Why not?"

He does not answer. He lights a cigarette and his cadaverous hand, covered with dark hairs, trembles.

"You're clearly misguided!" he sighs, finally. "Why on earth would I have killed this boy! He surely didn't have any money on him. And I don't need money. So? Unless you start mentioning sadism ... But the doctors who have examined me would disagree with you ... I have several vices, but not that one!"

"Have you ever been married?"

"Never." He is categorical, with a trace of bitterness in his voice.

"Have you had many affairs? Any mistresses?"

"I don't like women!"

Monsieur Froget looks at the portrait, then at the accused who is straightening his tie in front of a mirror. "Do you have any enemies in whose interest it would be to compromise you?"

Rodrigues hesitates, remains silent.

"Answer! You have led certain people to believe — and this is the general opinion in the world that you frequent — that Rodrigues is just a borrowed name, that you could have claimed a name that would have been significantly more important."

No reply. But the cigarette shifts from one corner of the lips to the other, without any manual help, then returns to its original position.

"Please sit down as you were sitting on Tuesday evening."

"I was not seated."

"Ah! You were standing for hours and hours?"

"Excuse me! At first, we drank in the room next door. We only came in here to get the opium pipes ..."

"And you smoked them standing up?"

"We went back to the other room."

"That was out of character! That was your opium den, wasn't it?"

"I don't see what you're getting at ..."

"Who prepared the pipes?"

"But ... everyone had their own ..."

"How many did S ... smoke?

"Six or seven ..."

"At what point did the argument begin?"

"There had been no argument and I warn you, there's no point in trying to outwit me ..."

Monsieur Froget walks towards the door, opens it and speaks to one of the two police officers. "Please bring me a police photographer. Warn him that he will have to reproduce a rather large portrait."

He remains in the first room where he carefully examines a

collection of miniature ships inside some bottles. By accident, he knocks over an African mask with pale eyes and crimson lips.

Rodrigues remained in the other half of the apartment. Finally, in the most natural way possible, the magistrate asks a question from where he is standing: "Is it done?"

Monsieur Froget heard the sound of a surprised person who was trying not to look disconcerted. He walks toward the door, notices the accused who holds in his hands a piece of the painting, which has been cut apart at face-level. He asks: "What's the rush? This portrait is based on a photograph, so the original must still be lying around somewhere?"

"I don't have it anymore ..."

"That's just what I thought."

Rodrigues is a bundle of nerves. Despite the darkness of his skin, one can discern a few irregular, red spots which seem to stain his cheeks as though he had been slapped across the face.

"Do you have anything to add?" Monsieur Froget says sharply without bothering to glance at him.

His clenched fingers rip the thin slices of canvas. On one of them, one can still see a big brown eye, with curved eyebrows.

The judge opens and shuts the drawers from a little dresser. He leaves one of them open, the one containing a revolver with a mother-of-pearl grip.

He leaves without looking at Rodrigues, enters the first room where, once again, he contemplates the three masts of the miniature ship through the green-tinted glass of the bottles.

✣ ✣ ✣

Monsieur Froget had just enough time to jot a few words down in his dime-store notebook. He wrote with such a pointed-edge fountain pen that in the hands of anyone else would have surely put a hole through the paper:

"*Proof.* S ..., who had never been initiated into the world of drugs, smokes six to seven opium pipes and prepares these very pipes himself. (Rodrigues's testimony).

"Impossible! But Rodrigues feels the need to establish that S ... was still alive when he left the room with the window panes in order to hide the importance of the portrait.

"*Assumptions*: the *concierge*'s deposition. Traces of blood. A cut on the hand. Rodrigues spontaneously declares that he walked his guest home in the opposite direction from the Seine; insists on his being drunk. Maintains that the *soirée* had taken place in the living room with the portrait in it, then retracts this statement.

"*The portrait's role.* Twenty years old, just like Rodrigues' wealth, just like his obsession with aristocracy. The original destroyed, or *returned to an interested party*. Obviously torn during the night of the crime. Disfigured as soon as it is supposed to be photographed.

"This is at the heart of the crime. Because if Rodrigues had committed premeditated murder, he would have done it on the quay itself, instead of taking the dangerous and painful risk of carrying the body himself.

"He attracted S ... to his house, however. S ... had humiliated him. He insisted on bringing him before the portrait of the *naked* woman, despite the fact that he was in the room next door."

At that moment, Monsieur Froget heard the detonation of a gun deep in the apartment, and he let out a satisfied sigh.

✤ ✤ ✤

Much later, in the smoking room of Monsieur Froget's Champ-de-Mars apartment. Monsieur Froget was surrounded by three magistrates and a psychiatrist.

"A boy who did not like women," the judge said, "who, while in Spain, purposefully seduced the daughter of a high-level official within the Foreign Affairs office where he worked, but who must have finally given up on his unsuccessful marriage and settled for a sum of money in exchange for, among other things, an excessively compromising portrait.

"He is consumed by his situation. It eats him up. He is neither an aristocrat nor a peasant ...

"The newspapers tell him all about the one who has become a duchess, about her husband, about her son. He looks at that portrait which he had wanted to be in the nude, not for the sake of sensuality, but to strip it of any ounce of prestige.

"One day, he meets the son in Paris. The young man makes fun of him, treats him as beneath his notice.

"And so Rodrigues hatches a diabolical plan, inspired by twenty years of unquenched ambition.

"Place the son in front of the portrait when he is half drunk ...

"After this moral crime, he needed to commit a physical one, in order to protect himself."

And without the slightest transition, Monsieur Froget placed a bridge game onto the table.

The Third Culprit

MADAME SMITT

MADAME SMITT

IT STOOD just three hundred meters from the Porte d'Orléans metro station. It was a two-story, dirty brick house, surrounded by a garden, which in winter was nothing more than a puddle of mud from which the branches of the bushes emerged.

To the right of the door, which was pierced with a spy hole, an enamel plaque read: *Family Boarding House — Moderate Prices*.

Monsieur Froget entered the premises on December 11, 1929 and was greeted by a red-headed girl, whose face was sprinkled with freckles and who was wiping her hands, which were bloated with chilblains.

There was nothing but chaos. The flooring tiles in the hallways were muddy. On the right, there was a dining room, with eight tables covered with tablecloths and opened bottles of beer. It smelled like a pharmacy.

A young man came tearing down the staircase and left without looking at the judge.

"A boarder?"

"Yes. There are only three left. The others are all gone."

"Is Madame Smitt feeling better?"

"She's doing very badly. She says she's going to die."

"Take me to her."

The room was neither on the first or second floor, but rather in a freezing attic, which was hardly furnished at all, and which one could enter only by a hallway that was cluttered with the boarders' trunks. The servant answered one of the judge's questions with: "You see !

Madame Smitt prefers to rent the rooms and sleep here ..."

Crudely illuminated by a light that came straight from a gable window, the landlady was in bed. She was so thin that one had a difficult time making out the curves of her body underneath the red covers. Her hair was in a bun, but in disarray, half-undone. She had a yellow face with feverish eyes which glared cantankerously at the judge. Her shoulders were barely any bigger than those of a child.

"Are you feeling any better?"

She began to cough. At first, she might have been faking it. But the coughing fit came and she had a devil of a time catching her breath. After which, without answering, she gave Froget a look which seemed to say: "This is what you're responsible for!"

The doctor determined that her condition, while not hopeless, was serious enough. A cold spell had sent her to bed for more than a day, when she expected it the least. It happened on December 6th exactly.

On the 8th, a boarder, a waiter in a café in Montparnasse, found a dead dog in the garden that some urchins had thrown over the hedges. He had started to dig a hole in the ground in order to bury the carcass. He had been completely stupefied when he uncovered human remains. He had called the police immediately.

Ever since, each day brought a little surprise. And, of course, Madame Smitt's condition worsened and worsened. She received the detectives with her teeth clenched, but looked at them with a stare that was as sharp as a stiletto knife. She had always been thin, servile, with a somewhat indefinable attitude — something that was both obsequious and terribly energetic.

She owned the house. She ran it herself. She employed only one maid and she worked from dawn to dusk. Her boarders were mostly English or American. Despite being so close to Montparnasse, she rarely had any artists or students. More and more, her boarding house catered to jugglers, chorus boys and people without any precise profession.

Of course, the Criminal Records Office had taken possession of the body, which they had subjected to every possible examination. Their field of inquiry was limited, however, as the body had been dead for at least five years.

The report read :

The deceased, who is of medium build, was killed by a fracture of the skull. At the time of his burial, he was wearing striped cotton pyjamas. There were no particular clues to be found. He must have been around thirty-five to forty-years old.

Madame Smitt answered all of the questions with hateful looks. One hardly had time to formulate a sentence before she would cry out: "I know nothing!"

The telephone and the telegraph were working and, as is often the case, it became clear that the seemingly insignificant Porte d'Orléans house had been hiding a much more troublesome activity than one had imagined.

Madame Smitt's origins were looked into, for example. Her neighbors had taken her for a very meritorious widow, for an energetic woman who had fallen on hard times. Yet, Scotland Yard had responded to a questionnaire sent by Froget with the following cablegram:

```
Natalie Esther Grant, the daughter of a
clergyman from Kent. At the age of sixteen,
runs away from home to London in order to
follow a music-hall clown who promptly
```

abandons her. She was a quick learner. Was hired by a commercial firm. Five years later, marries the vice-president, Richard Hollaway, who handles her business affairs. Halloway becomes an associate at Grimborn and Mower. Starts a working-class clothes manufacturing business, which doesn't turn a profit. Very disappointing bank statements. No credit.

Just when bankruptcy seemed inevitable, someone who had just withdrawn cash from his account turned up dead in the Thames. The police trace the victim all the way back to the Halloway-Grimborn-Mower trio, to the store where it had been discovered that the murder had taken place.

The crime occurred on January 25, 1914. Extraordinarily, the payee only had 30,000 francs on him which were still missing.

Halloway confesses, is sentenced to twenty years of hard labor; Grimborn is sentenced to the same, and Mower gets ten years. Halloway dies of consumption in 1919. Grimborn is still in prison. Mower had been released, in 1923, after an accident which cost him his right eye.

The police know nothing about Mrs. Hollaway, except that her complicity had not been established and that she had left England as soon as the trial was over. But she resurfaces at the town hall of the fourteenth *arrondissement* in Paris, where, in 1921, she marries a certain John Smitt, a British subject and commercial traveler.

At this time, she does not yet own her boarding house. She works for an Australian company in Paris. She doesn't move to her Porte d'Orléans residence until a year later, with half of the house paid for in cash, or thirty thousand francs to be exact, and the rest to be paid for from annuities.

During the first days of the investigation, Madame Smitt had been asked questions about her second husband.

"In short, he disappeared immediately after your marriage. Why?"

"I have no idea."

"Where did you meet him?"

No answer. Based on her mute responses, some police officers conclude that the body and John Smitt are one and the same. But Monsieur Froget remains silent, places an announcement in the newspaper, urging the said John Smitt to come forth or to write to the Seine Prosecutor's Office.

On the 9th of December, a letter from Boulogne arrives, signed by Smitt who alleges that he simply cannot go to Paris unless a warrant is issued for his arrest. He's a down-and-out. He says he's a docker — but he is in fact as much a docker as he had been a sales representative. When he met Mrs. Halloway, he was a sandwich-man. She offered him a thousand francs to marry her and to go away afterwards.

"She needed my name!" he said cynically, but with no real understanding of the scheme he hoped to profit from.

❖ ❖ ❖

Madame Smitt's illness becomes even more useful to her now that it is authentic. Her fever oscillates between 39 and 39.8 degrees celsius. To see her lying down, one wonders how, just eight days earlier, she was able to come and go freely at home.

True, this was a question that was frequently asked. She had always been weak, sickly. The people in her neighborhood would say of her: "She's a poor woman who hasn't got two cents worth of health to her, but who gallops about town all day anyway!"

And a few boarders, who sometimes took pity on her, would take the broom or the cleaning rags right out her hands.

As she lay in bed, her smile was the pathetic smile of a victim. Hadn't the entire world conspired against her? Against a frail creature who had been worn out by sickness and who never ceased to be tested and proven!

Monsieur Froget coughed, mechanically.

The red-headed maid takes leave but not without sending a disdainful look his way, as though he were an executioner. In the room below, a boarder, a saxophone player, needs to continue practicing despite everything. A strange sort of metallic wails rise from one floor to another.

"Do you have enough strength to answer a few questions?"

She remains silent, though smiling. And one should not be afraid of being accused of being cold-hearted by staying there after such a smile!

"Why did you spend a thousand francs to change your name in 1921 even though you seemed keen on money at that time?"

She coughs to the point of losing her breath, and momentarily turns scarlet.

"Nobody in France was aware of your husband's conviction. The past could not have affected you in any way as a result of this. It was the marriage, on the other hand, which was dangerous."

She looked at him with a certain amount of concern.

"I repeat: dangerous. Because, a little later, you would buy a house.

As a married woman, you had no choice but to buy it in your husband's name. You needed his signature ... I know ... you needed him to put his signature on all sorts of stamped documents ... That not withstanding, if he had wanted to, he could have demanded his share of the building ..."

A pair of surprisingly cold and lucid eyes stared at the magistrate. Thin lips remained frozen. The face is yellow and pink, a sickly apple-cheeked pink.

"How many years have you had a maid?"

She answers no further. He consults his notebook.

"The one you are currently employing was hired in 1927. Before that, you had a maid from Brittany, who began working for you in 1926. And yet, the crime occurred around 1924 when you only had a housekeeper come in three or four hours a day ..."

Madame Smitt has shut her eyes and her mouth, slightly ajar, allows for only the most difficult of breaths.

"Under those conditions, it was easy for you to dig a hole in your garden, and shove a corpse in it as soon as the boarders had left for the day."

Silence. A sliver of a melody that the saxophone player attempts to begin three times and which ends in a sort of burst of incongruous laughter.

"From 1921 to 1925, Smitt wrote to you from time to time, from Marseilles, from Bordeaux, from Calais, to ask you for little sums of money. You would send him ten francs at a time. From 1925 onwards you no longer answered his letters."

"I had had enough ..."

She extends her arm towards a glass of water which had been placed onto the table. Monsieur Froget puts the glass in her hands. She avidly downs her glass and allows her head to rest on her pillow. "Are you finished now? ..."

Her entire face is tormented. One could suppose that any minute could be her last breath. Monsieur Froget is cold. He turns his head, as the old woman is still coughing, seemingly without end. He frowns as the saxophone player starts another piece with an exasperating slowness.

"Who owns the dumb-bells that were found in the courtyard?"

"They belong to a boarder who left them behind ..."

"Mower was blind in his left eye, was he not?"

"The right eye ...Wait ...Yes ..."

"When did you see him for the last time?"

"Two days before ... before the ... incident, in 1914 ... he was dining at our house ... Give me another glass of water ..."

"He never wrote to you?"

"Once, in 1926 or 27: a simple postcard, from Canada, he wrote down his signature only."

"Was it a postcard of a big city?"

"No ... wait... a frozen river, I think.."

"Mower didn't ask you for any money?"

"No ... some water ... I can't take it anymore ..."

Monsieur Froget filled the glass, handed it to her, left the room after one last glance at the old woman who was not drinking but who, as she sat on her bed, followed him nervously with her eyes.

Madame Smitt poisoned herself the day after having been transferred to the Saint-Lazare infirmary, under circumstances which could never be explained. The only document of any use was Monsieur Froget's notebook from which I copied the following lines:

✠ ✠ ✠

"Madame Smitt is guilty of Mower's murder.

"*Proof*: Madame Smitt states that Mower is blind in his right eye.

And yet he became blind in prison. She therefore saw him after he was released from prison, which she denies.

"*Assumptions:* She spends a thousand francs in order to marry Smitt despite the serious perils of such a manoeuver, while everyone in France has no knowledge of her past. Then it is not the authorities she wishes to flee *but someone who would be looking for her.* And it is for this reason that she officially changes her name.

"This is how things played out: Mrs. Halloway holds on to the 30,000 francs that were stolen from the murdered man. Goes to France. Keeps the money. Her husband dies. Grimborn is locked up for twenty years. But Mower will soon be let out of prison. He is entitled to a share of that amount. In order to avoid sharing anything, she changes her marital status by marrying Smitt. Moves to the suburbs. Buys a house under her new name. Once free, Mower catches up with her anyway. She feigns submissiveness. Offers him her hospitality. Makes him drink or fills him up with a narcotic. That night, she sneaks into his room as he sleeps and beats him to death with the dumb-bells.

"Under *no* circumstances will she sell her house in order to give any part of it over to Mower."

And, in red ink in the margins:

"A classic case of someone desperately trying to hang on to ill-gotten profits."

The Fourth Culprit

THE "FLEMINGS"

THE "FLEMINGS"

IT WAS the first time that Monsieur Froget had come into contact with a seventy-two year old suspect and it was likely that, perhaps from the very beginning of the case, he was impressed by him. Even though he had not yet looked him in the face, he abruptly pronounced: "Would you blow your nose, I beg of you!"

The man's name was Baas. He was one of those human specimens that city people always seem to forget, but that in the past one could find at least one example in each village: a formidable build, a chest like a trunk, almost as thick as it was large, and the whole was sculpted in a hard and lead-like material. A bear!

Half of Baas's face was covered with grayish hair, three to four centimeters in length. He was sitting nervously on the edge of his chair, with his hat on his knees, ready, one could say, to leap at the first sign of danger.

While the magistrate was flipping through the files, he kept his eyes shut for the most part. But his eye lids would lift from time to time and a most piercing gaze would emerge that would strike Froget within the span of a second. A cold, worrisome stare that one finds in certain very evolved animals.

He wiped his nostrils with the back of his hand and paused, inhaling and batting his eyelashes. His lips were drawn. One could feel him saying to himself: "He's clever! ... They're all clever, in there! ... And they're going to try to fool me! ... But we'll see about that ..."

And his entire body stiffened up. He pushed prudence to the limits, to the point where he made his shutter-like eyelids close onto his reddish pupils.

The crime had been committed that very night. In the morning, Monsieur Froget had gone down to the crime scene at Aubervilliers, accompanied by the prosecutor and some experts. It was now and would be henceforth the most bitter memory of his career. A nightmare, in every sense of the word.

Leaving Paris, crossing the lively suburbs, arriving in Aubervilliers' culture and factories and noticing, far from any house, a shanty in the middle of the fields: a cube. The inhabitants were uncomfortable when one brought up the "Flemings." They speak of the hovel with embarrassment and one of them felt the need to say eloquently: "We don't even know how many of them are in there, nor who's producing the urchins who are growing there! ..."

There were four rooms, a stable, nooks and corners filled with manure and agricultural instruments. Chickens, dogs, cats and children, a hodgepodge, blended within the filth. Three women, a fifty-year old, a twenty-two-year old and a sixteen-year old. Then there was Baas, shuffling noiselessly through the dark rooms, creeping, slithering, spying, elusive.

In a bedroom, to the right, a corpse, that one might mistake for Baas himself if Baas hadn't been right there looking at him. Same build. Same age. But with a useless head. The doctor counts ... thirty one ... thirty two ... thirty three blows from the hammer ... And no one cries! Nothing but dry eyes, snarling faces, words whispered in Flemish.

When the questioning begins, out comes a vague jumble of words, a pile of contradictions, and answers such as: "Maybe ... That could be ... How should I know?" You prove to people that they're lying and they couldn't care less. They just make up another story, with the same thoughtlessness. Thoughtlessness? The word demands to be repeated almost obsessively to the point where one could be transported hundreds of years in the past, to an era of obscurantism and amorality. One can hardly determine whose children they are. The sixteen-year old girl is the mother of the latest one. And there's no point in even mentioning the existence of a father!

Monsieur Froget was so accurate in sensing that things would only get murkier and murkier, not only on a daily basis, but on an hourly one, that he rushed back to his office and made sure Baas was brought in at once.

The women are being watched on the spot. This doesn't seem to bother them, not any more than the corpse did. At noon, they ate a great big helping of potatoes in a sour milk sauce.

✤ ✤ ✤

Establishing the Flemings' exact identity is already a daunting task. Almost no documents at all, only, a Belgian military service record and a birth certificate. For better or for worse, however, Monsieur Froget starts some files, in front of Baas, who opens and closes his eyes with almost rhythmic regularity.

> *Baas*, Jean-Joseph-Alphonse, born in Neeroeteren (of the Belgian Limbourg region), agricultural worker. Three years of military service, in the Second Lancers division at Arlon. Sets off to America. Returns ten years later with twenty thousand francs and meets van Straelen. A real brute. With a full beard.
>
> *Van Straelen*, Pieter-Auguste, born in Neeroeteren, a journeyman. Carried out his military service in the same regiment as Baas. Settled near Argenteuil where he rented some land. Got married a few years later to a woman twenty years younger then he. She had a gorilla's figure. Snub-nosed.

Emma van Straelen, born in Tongres, a brasserie waitress, up until the day she met van Straelen in the Les Halles district of Paris and marries him.

Céline, their oldest daughter, twenty-two years old, mother of three children whom Baas fathered, according to local gossip.

Louise, the youngest daughter, sixteen-years old. Baas would be the father of this child as well.

When Baas came back from America with money he had earned in the mines, he began to seek out van Straelen, his childhood friend. He found him in Argenteuil. He moved in with him. At first, he helped out with the work.

Then the Aubervilliers shack went up for sale. Baas bought it. Van Straelen was, in fact, just a farmer.

But, in practice, the situation was much less cut and dry. No one kept any records at all. Baas lived there without doing anything. Van Straelen worked his land. And it was Emma who, at three o'clock every morning, harnessed the horse and brought the vegetables to the covered market in Les Halles.

When Céline gave birth to her first child, Baas deposited a thousand francs in a savings account in his name at the Caisse d'Epargne bank. And the same was done for the rest, including Louise's child. But Céline was the only one to have her bed in Baas's room. Everyone else slept in the same room and a three-year-old urchin slept on the floor on a straw mattress.

Two years before, Baas had received a small inheritance, around ten thousand francs that he had put in the bank. He was totally illiterate and signed his name with an X. It was van Straelen who, knowing how to read and write himself, took care of most of the paperwork.

The "Flemings"

One question provoked contradictory answers: "Did you also have relations with Emma van Straelen?"

There were yes's and no's, some maybe's and some vague gestures.

One fact was certain: van Straelen was jealous of neither his wife nor his girls. Baas had all the power. Everything was his: the house and its hosts. And all this had continued for thirty years in Aubervilliers, an hour away from Paris by tram, with little contact with the civilized world, so to speak, nor even with the century itself. To the point where Baas did not speak French but a pidgin language made up of Flemish, Spanish and slang.

The neighbors knew nothing of this. From time to time, they saw Baas pass by, silent and heavy, and swinging his arms like a large monkey. As for van Straelen, one saw him only from afar, hunched over in his fields, laboring with a single-minded obstinacy, and always alone. All anyone knew was that the Fleming bought several liters of gin every week and that van Straelen played the accordion once in a while, in the evenings, at his doorstep.

The previous night at nine o'clock, the Flemings went off to bed, in a disorganized fashion. At three o'clock, Emma had already left with the cart. When she came home, at ten o'clock, Baas and Céline were busy looking at the corpse. At least two hours had gone by since they had discovered it, but they had waited for the woman before calling the police. Each of them had claimed that they knew nothing, saw nothing, heard nothing.

It took this crime to reveal that this same van Straelen who had been found murdered, had been sick for seven weeks, paralyzed in his bed. As it was winter, the neighboring villagers had not noticed that he was absent from his fields. His family had neglected to call a doctor.

"He was dying, for goodness sake!" Emma said. "And, since he was whimpering all the time, we had put up a bed in a poor room. From time to time, someone came over to check up on him."

After the autospy, the coroner concluded that, even if he had not been killed, van Straelen would have lived only two or three days. That wasn't the least of it, this murderous fixation on an inert body at death's door who, moreover, was no longer in command of his faculties! Thirty-three hammer blows! One might as well have said that he no longer had a head. The weapon had not been found yet. A well had to be emptied; several swamps needed to be dried up.

"How did the criminal come in?"

"Through the door! When Emma leaves, nobody gets up to bolt it ..."

The autopsy had revealed that the crime had been committed between six and seven o'clock in the morning, so that Emma, who at that moment had been at the Halles, was the only one not under suspicion.

The stunned children, who should have been interrogated, burst into tears or babbled a few inchoate syllables.

✛ ✛ ✛

Baas was now seated in one of those booths in the Palais de Justice, crushing his chair with his own weight, trembling each time Monsieur Froget made the slightest movement.

His nose was running once more and, as he did not seem to notice it, the magistrate clicked his fingers impatiently. "Blow your nose!"

He obeyed, his eyes full of spite.

"Did Baas shave often?"

He had to repeat the question. And yet, Monsieur Froget felt that the man had understood him. At first, he answered: " On occasion ..." Then:

The "Flemings"

"On Saturdays ..."

"Who was the last one to shave him? ..."

And he was forced to repeat once more, as he hammered each syllable: "Me ... and Emma ... the other week ..."

"Shaved him so well, in fact, that no other stranger needed to set foot in the house ..."

Against his usual pattern, Froget lit another cigarette. Redness surrounded Baas's eyes, his limp lips came down over his toothless mouth. He had a mixture of exceptional strength and decrepitude. And that cold stare which filtered through, extinguished, and then cautiously emerged once more.

"Van Straelen owned nothing?"

"Nothing ..."

"Didn't he have any life insurance?"

This time, Froget had to listen to an entire explanation. It was as though each question went on forever.

"No ..."

"At what time do you normally get up in the morning?"

"At six o'clock ... seven ..."

"And Céline?"

"The same ..."

"She stated that she got up at eight o'clock ..."

"That's possible ..."

"Was it Louise who discovered the body?"

"Could very well be ..."

"You said this morning that you were the one ..."

"So what! ..."

Baas grumbled at length before each word. His hands bulging with veins, his skin caked with earth, were placed on his knees. The shape of his joints was no longer recognizable. Two of his nails were blackened to the root.

The telephone rang resoundingly. One of the detectives who had stayed in the shack announced that the wells had been emptied without result.

"Are the women still saying nothing?"

"The old woman asked if she could still go to the Halles tonight. She's talking about some cabbage that might spoil ..."

"And the youngest?"

"She's ironing some laundry ..."

"Céline?"

"She cried ... she comes and goes in and out of the house ... You can tell she's got some sort of weight on her shoulders."

Monsieur Froget hung up the phone, stared at Baas who, during this questioning, kept his eyes shut.

"Give me the summons!" the magistrate finally said to his clerk.

He took the piece of paper, handed it to the old man, pointing out the bottom of the page to him with his hand. With his other hand, he offered him a fountain pen.

"What must I write down?

"Sign ..."

Baas squashed a X down on the paper.

"Blow your nose!"

✣ ✣ ✣

Monsieur Froget wrote down a few words on a form, pushed the paper towards the suspect, without lifting his head, and, in a neutral voice, announced: "Here is the warrant for your arrest, van Straelen ..."

The hand with the bulging veins took the piece of paper. It was trembling. And, as the murderer read, Monsieur Froget wrote, but slowly this time, in minuscule inky letters, on a page in his notebook:

"*Proofs* — 1. The suspect fell right into the trap that I had set for him, when I asked him: 'Did Baas shave often?' — His answer: 'From time to time' exposed him. He forgets that he wants to pass himself off as Baas.

"2. The suspect asked *what he should write down.* And yet, Baas could neither read nor write.

"3. The same man who paid no attention to his appearance, bothered to shave the dying man, who, by the way, had never been washed or cared for and wallowed in his own filth. *Yet, Baas's beard was the most striking difference between the two Flemish men*

"4. None of them had opened their mouths, including Emma van Straelen, because it was in *everyone's interest.*

"*Asssumptions or Clues.* — Baas, who was sick, was going to die any day. Yet, everything belonged to Baas. For thirty years, the family had lived exclusively on Baas's money.

"The two men were the same height, the same age. The neighbors could barely distinguish the two.

"Shaving the dying man, finishing him off, and disfiguring him completely with hammer blows, passing him off as van Straelen; and van Straelen became Baas, the owner of the shack, of the fields and of the money that was deposited into the bank account.

"This was premeditated since, for weeks, he had to let his beard grow."

Monsieur Froget looked at the man who stood before him in a curious manner, with his drooping lip, his dead eyes, with a little wetness around his eyelids. And so, he jotted down in the margins, before curtly closing his notebook: "Motive: the land."

The Fifth Culprit

NOUCHI

NOUCHI

MONSIEUR FROGET handled this case with a certain amount of nonchalance which brought a grin to many people.

If Nouchi did not fit textbook definitions of beauty, she was certainly alluring and extraordinarily young. Nineteen-years old to be exact. She had a long, firm body, with high little breasts which she sculpted as much as possible within her silk dress, which was so light that she could have held it in the palm of her hand. She had a narrow head which seemed as greasy as her black hair, parted in the middle of her head, stuck to her skull. She had brown eyes. A wet mouth.

And that painfully sought after elegance, which was fundamentally strange and which reeked of *Mitteleuropa* a mile away. Nouchi was Hungarian. But she had lived in Paris with her mother and sister for several years and spoke French with just the right amount of spice.

She conducted herself with calm effrontery. During her first cross-examination, hadn't she interrupted the judge in order to ask: "Would you have a cigarette, by any chance?"

She sat with her legs crossed, while revealing at length her nervous thighs.

Eleven examinations in six days. Only one of them, the first one, dealt with meat of the interrogation. Nouchi had been accused of having entered Mrs. Crosby's premises, with whom she had become friendly, in the owner's absence, and of having stolen a pearl necklace worth a half a million.

She had left some magnificent fingerprints on the writing desk, where the jewel in question had been locked up. Monsieur Froget had the enlarged photographs of them before his eyes. Each of the fingers was precisely laid out before him, without flaws: long fingers among which the last digit was strangely bent.

Mrs. Crosby and her insurance company were becoming increasingly impatient, and phoned the *Parquet*[1] as often as three times a day.

Monsieur Froget, who had loosened up a little bit, gave the impression of being like a gentleman tasting the pleasures of a walk in the country. The truth of the matter was that it was useless for Nouchi to risk a more audacious flirtation, such as readjusting her garter belt or nestling up right next to the magistrate. He would not get angry. Only, he had a smile that disarmed her, that forced her to return to her seat blushing.

What Nouchi found really exasperating, however, was that he kept on returning to the same questions and that she searched fruitlessly for some sort of trap. That eleventh examination, for example, began: "In Budapest, you lived in a big house, I believe?"

"A big house, yes! With many servants. And as I've already told you, my father was a State Counselor. Do you really want me to repeat last week's lesson every time, just like in grade school? My father died shortly after the war, when I was still very young. My mother sold everything. And since we were ruined financially, she preferred to hide out in Paris ... You haven't forgotten our address have you? 23, rue des Saints-Pères. Two hotel rooms with connecting doors ..." In exasperation, she pretended to be a star student reciting a lesson.

---

[1]The Public Prosecutor's Department.

Nouchi

"Your mother doesn't speak French?"

"All right, if you're bringing up *maman*, I can see what you're getting at! Fifty French words, which she learned in high school, thirty years ago. Insisted on speaking French with *Papa* nonetheless, because it was considered chic. No doubt, you'd like me to tell you that she's a bit silly, that she dresses like a little girl, colors her hair like a blonde Venetian, hosts receptions in our rooms as though we lived in a chateau? ... My friends claim that she's slightly mad ..."

"And your sister?"

"A younger version of my mother ...She'll become *maman* in forty years ... she embroiders, she cries, she takes piano lessons and she reads poetry ..."

"So well in fact that the entire household lives off your earnings?"

"And a very small annuity, yes ..."

"Who gave you the idea to draw fashion sketches for the newspapers?"

"Me! I don't need other people's ideas."

"How much do you make?"

"The months when we're presenting the fashion shows, from two to four thousand francs ... the other months, practically nothing ..."

"Your mother gave you a considerable amount of freedom?"

"You got it! I frequented the bars in Montparnasse. And I had friends. And I often went out with Siveschi whom you know and who is a salesman in a record store on the avenue Montaigne!"

"Was there not something else between you two that ... ?"

"Bring in the doctor and he'll tell you!"

She didn't even bother to give her answers some thought. Answers flew out of her mouth even before the questions were fully articulated. From time to time, she got up, walked around the office and sat back down, sometimes on the edge of Monsieur Froget's desk.

"You must understand. When I say friend, I mean friend. And the day I mean lover, I'll say lover ... but it'll never be Siveschi ..."

"Where did you meet Mrs. Crosby?"

"At the fashion shows ... She attended them as though she were a client, and I as a sketch artist ... One day, we started chatting ... Then we had tea together ..."

"She's much older than you are, however, isn't she?"

"Thirty-five years older. That should be written somewhere in your papers. Her husband is a multi-millionaire, but old and annoying. And so she leaves him in Chicago and she travels through Europe ..."

"Did you visit her often at her apartment on the rue François-1er?"

"Almost every day ... But don't get the wrong idea ... Mrs. Crosby — Ellen, as I called her in the end — likes men, I swear to you ..."

"Precisely! It seems as though you would do little favors for her when she was having an affair ..."

"Little ones, yes ..."

"Did she often give you money"

"Sometimes ... she was very generous ... She would leave money around all the time ... And if she had had a few cocktails, she would give you a thousand francs as easily as a hundred ... unless of course she got angry, for no reason, and cursed at you! ... This ring is a gift from her."

She offered her left hand. The ring, incidentally, was the only blemish that one could see on the enlarged pictures of the fingerprints.

"Was Mrs. Crosby ever at your mother's?"

"Once! ... It wasn't an experience that made her feel like coming back. Mrs. Crosby drank on an empty stomach ... My mother wanted to imitate her and she got sick ... she cried ... she complained in Hungarian ... it was loads of fun, I can assure you! ..."

"Did Mrs. Crosby show you her necklace herself?"

"Yes! She added that, if her husband had given it to her, it wasn't out of niceness, but for a calculated reason ... In America, you have the good sense to think of everything, and, even if you have tens of millions of dollars, you're still planning for potential ruin ... In the end, that necklace was just there for a rainy day ..."

"How many pearls were there?"

"I have no idea ..."

"The theft took place on Tuesday, the eleventh of June, is that correct?"

"Possibly! I no longer keep track of the days ..."

"That morning, you went to the rue François-1er and you lunched with Mrs. Crosby ... You then accompanied her to the Saint-Lazare train station, as she was going to spend two days in Deauville ... is that right?"

"Absolutely ..."

"What did you do after that?"

"I went home and I wanted to work ... My mother was out with my sister."

"So no one saw you?"

"Excuse-me! I cut my hand sharpening a pencil. Blood was running so hard that I got frightened and I called the bellboy ... he helped me make a bandage ... I'm still wearing it in fact ..." She presented her right index finger, wrapped up in a pink gummy strip.

"What time was it then?"

"Four o'clock ... I noticed that I had left one of my sketch books at the rue François-1er apartment ... It was impossible for me to work without the papers it contained ... I went back there and the chambermaid let me in ..."

"Did she follow you into the apartment?"

"No! She knew that Mrs. Crosby trusted me."

"Did you go into the bedroom where the writing table was?"

"Yes! But I didn't stay there long, because I remembered that, that morning, I hadn't set foot into that room ... And, in fact, it was in the boudoir that I found my notebook."

"You didn't touch the writing desk at all?"

"No ..."

"And yet your fingerprints were all over it!"

She merely shrugged her shoulders.

"How much time did you spend in the apartment?"

"A half an hour ..."

"That's indeed what the chambermaid said. A half an hour just to look for a sketchbook ..."

"I was tired and I sat down in an armchair ... I read a short story in an English magazine that was lying around ..."

"Did you go home right afterwards?"

"You know that I didn't. That was when Siveschi left work ... I waited for him at the door ... we went for a drink in Montparnasse."

"You didn't go to his place?"

"No ..."

"You didn't come home before nine o'clock? What did you do until then?"

Silence.

"How much did Siveschi make per month?"

"A thousand francs ..."

"And he spends fifteen to sixteen hundred ..."

Nouchi

"That's his business ... Arrest him!"

Monsieur Froget picked up the phone.

"Hello! Elysée 37-07 please ... Yes! Ask for Mrs. Crosby ..."

Nouchi frowned. And this was all that was needed to add an unexpected harshness to her face. "What do you want to do?"

"A question! Are you sure that you didn't injure your hand while trying to break into the writing desk? ... It had brass brackets ... it would only take a wrong move ..."

"I told you that I hurt myself with a pocket knife, at the rue Saint-Pères ... the floor waiter witnessed it ... all you have to do is bring him in here ..."

The phone rings.

"Hello! ... Mrs. Crosby? ... Would you be so kind as to hop into a cab and come by my office? ... No! Nothing new to speak of ... It's just a simple formality ..."

And Nouchi asked, in a voluble manner: "What formality? What did I say? ... You have to admit that you know nothing and that ..."

Monsieur Froget, who was barely smiling, pushed something towards her.

✛ ✛ ✛

What Monsieur Froget had slid into the young lady's hand was the picture of the fingerprints for her ten fingers, where one noticed but one irregularity caused by the ring on the left ring finger.

"This is my proof," he said almost benevolently. "You were not wounded then when you voluntarily placed your fingerprints onto the writing desk And so this transaction took place not in the afternoon, at which point you would have been wearing a bandage that would have left a mark, but in the morning. Therefore in Mrs. Crosby's presence. So ... how much did she promise you in exchange for your being a suspect for a few days?"

Nouchi shot a hateful look his way. Monsieur Froget had already opened his notebook, which was a habit that bordered on a tic, and wrote the following down on a blank page:

"*Assumptions*: — 1. If Nouchi had stolen, knowing that she would be a suspect, she would not have openly waited for Siveschi by the entrance of his workplace.

2. She would have made sure that her evening corresponded to a plausible and indisputable plan.

3. She reacted and answered the questioning as though she *wanted to be accused*.

Mrs. Crosby arrived busily, all silk and perfume. "Do you need a signature from me?"

"Later, yes, madame. On the prison registry ... It is an honor to charge you with attempted fraud against the Company that insured your jewels."

And, as the American, suddenly stiffened, turned furiously towards Nouchi, Froget calmly added: "She honestly played her role up to the very end. You must admit that she is not responsible for having cut her hand. Would you be so kind as to answer two questions? First: what did you do with the false pearls that replaced the ones that were sold by you a long time ago?

"I threw them into the sea, at Deauville ..."

"Thank you! How much did you offer Mademoiselle Nouchi to distract the Courts for a certain period of time and to avoid anyone's guessing the truth?"

"Fifty thousand ..." Mrs. Crosby blurted out.

And Froget, who remained impassive, saw Nouchi tense up, her fists clenched, her lips trembling.

Nouchi

"Fifty thousand? ... Five thousand, *monsieur le juge*! ... And ... and ... here! ... the glitter of this ring is also fake ..."

It was a minute before the hour. If the guard, who had just been summoned, had not arrived, the affair would have ended in a flurry of slaps and cat-like scratches.

The Sixth Culprit

ARNOLD SCHUTTRINGER

ARNOLD SCHUTTRINGER

"ABOVE ALL, *monsieur le juge*, I would like to declare ..."
"Nothing! You will answer my questions!"
Monsieur Froget let these words drop with a terrific calm. And, during the entire questioning, he remained frozen, with his shoulders unevenly positioned, his head in his white, almost waxen hand.

Arnold Schuttringer did not take his big goggle eyes off him. His eyes inspired a certain amount of ill will, even a strange kind of revulsion. Thirty-years old. Five foot eight. He looked a little too well nourished, or, more precisely, too bloated. His lips were characteristic. The edges were thick and strong. They looked like a piece of fruit ready to burst. There was something unhealthy, however, about his complexion. It was too white, despite the pink in his cheeks which made one suspect a bit of make-up. Very short, blond hair. His eyebrows were thin. His gray suit was too tight and pinched him all over and made his muscles seem puffy.

Hunched over his papers, Monsieur Froget spoke as though he were reading from a carefully studied text. "You were born in Zurich, from a German father and an Austrian mother, is that correct? Stop me only if I make a mistake. You studied Chemistry first at the University of Nuremberg. When you were twenty-three years old, you changed your mind and entered medical school in Bonn. Why did you suddenly decide to continue your studies in Paris?"

"Because, in Bonn, which was almost exclusively a college town, it was hard for me to make a living and study at the same time."

"Your parents didn't send you any money?"

"My father died ten years earlier, and my mother, who found work as a governess for an English family, earned just enough money to support herself."

"What made you go into medicine?"

"Personal reasons."

"You have declared on several occasions that you had no intention of practicing."

"That's true. I am a laboratory man."

"And you volunteered to do preparations for the lecture-hall. In other words, you were the one who cut up the bodies that were to be dissected."

"That's also true."

"Two years ago, you were employed, at night, at the *Pharmacie Central*, on the place Blanche. You started your shift at eight o'clock in the evening and you left at eight o'clock in the morning. The pharmacy was open 24 hours a day. You hardly ever showed up at the store itself. You had a tiny office with a cot. When an urgent prescription came in, the saleswoman would wake you up and you would go to the lab. Why did the owner of the pharmacy pick you over a pharmacist with a degree, and over a Frenchman?"

"Because I didn't mind working for half the normal salary. On the other hand, it was also understood that, during my shift, I was allowed to study and use the lab for my personal research."

"From eight to eight, you would study alone on the premises with Madame Joly, who worked in the store. At around one o'clock, she would make you some coffee which she would serve you in your office. You were her lover."

"That's what people say."

"One of the housekeepers, who came into work a little early one night, caught you *in flagrante.*"

"If that's what you want to believe."

" Madame Joly was thirty-five years old. Her husband was and still is a surveyor for an architectural firm. He's a man with a violent streak. He was very jealous and, for some time now, suspected what was going on. During the last couple of weeks, he showed up several times unexpectedly at night. Is this correct?"

"If you say so."

"At other times, Madame Joly noticed him in the street, loitering. He declared to his friends that some day you would both end up dead."

"I didn't know that."

"The night of the fifth or the six, you began your shift, as did Madame Joly, as usual. From evening to dawn, exactly thirteen customers came by, the cash register corroborates this. You were called upon to fill out prescriptions twice. At eleven thirty, Joly, who had gone to the movies, came by to see his wife and noticed you through the open door of your office. He did not greet you. At two o'clock in the morning, a cabaret dancer from the rue Pigalle showed up and waited for several minutes. She testified that the saleswoman finally arrived all disheveled and blushing very heavily."

Arnold curled his fleshy lips and grinned contemptuously: "Is that all?" he asked.

"Madame Joly usually left work at around seven o'clock, in order to be home before her husband woke up. You would be alone for about ten minutes, until the housekeepers arrived. On the fifth, she waited for the daytime employees and didn't leave the pharmacy before eight o'clock. You were asleep in your office. When the doors were opened, you pretended to emerge from a deep sleep."

"I appreciate your use of the word 'pretend'!" Schuttringer pronounced, sarcastically. "I suppose you think you're being scientific in reaching this conclusion?"

"When the employees arrived, Madame Joly had already put on her coat. She left on foot, towards the Place Clichy where she usually took the tram. You waited for the owner. After having exchanged a few words with him, you dropped by your house, on the rue Monsieur-le-Prince, then you went to the lecture hall."

He spoke in a flat monotone. Not one ounce of emotion. And there was no sense of combativeness either. On the one hand, an icy Monsieur Froget, reading from a prepared text; on the other, Schuttringer, staring at him with his big suspicious eyes.

"At nine o'clock, Monsieur Joly had been by the pharmacy to complain about not having seen his wife and asked for your address, which the owner did not dare give him, because of his agitated state. Out of desperation, he spent the entire morning looking for you in the various offices and rooms at the medical school. A young man who worked in the laboratory warned you just in time and you went out by a side door, and asked everyone not to give out your address. Do you acknowledge this?"

Arnold simply shrugged his shoulders.

"At five o'clock in the afternoon, an unexpected order that came in at the pharmacy forced a stock keeper to go down to the cellar. There, as he did not find what he was looking for, the man entered a "reserve" — a cellar that was smaller than the others in which dangerous products were kept such as the acids, among others things. Behind a row of candy boxes, he noticed some bags that were not in their proper place. He wanted to move them and cried out in pain. The gunny-bag was imbibed with vitriol. A little later, after the alarm was given, a body was discovered under the bags, cut up in three pieces and eaten away by sulfuric acid.

"You know what the autopsy concluded, don't you? The body had been dead for less than twenty-four hours. The shreds of clothing that survived corresponded to the clothes Mrs. Joly had worn the night before. Same age. Same height. Same weight. Monsieur Joly identified the body. He pointed the finger at you without hesitation and, if the police had not protected you, he would have killed you as soon as he could confront you.

"The pharmacy has only one entrance, doesn't it?" Arnold Schuttringer said slowly. "Let me point out to you that, moreover, I had absolutely nothing to gain by killing Madame Joly. Among other matters, there is one thing that your investigation did not uncover: which is, from the percentage that she earned from each sale, she gave me around two hundred francs per month." He said this with great calm. Not an ounce of embarrassment, nor human decency.

As though he had not heard the last sentences, Froget continued: "There is indeed another door. And, as of eight o'clock in the morning, there has always been someone in the pharmacy. Furthermore, we reconstructed your schedule on the day of the fifth and it was proven that you did not go to the Place Blanche."

"Which proves ..." began the accused, with sudden aggression.

But the answer that fell from Froget's lips with the thickness of hail, made him lose his assurance.

"Which proves nothing!"

✢ ✢ ✢

The silence which lasted five minutes seemed like an intermission. And, when the curtain rose, Arnold Schuttringer was less sure of himself. Monsieur Froget's attitude had also changed. His voice had more bite to it. His hands held an ivory paper cutter which he was bending so sharply that the suspect waited, mechanically, for the moment it would break.

"Please answer yes or no to the questions I must still ask you. In Bonn, you were involved in a public morals case in which the lives of a young seventeen-year old man and a sixteen-year old girl came to an end. Is this true?"

"One fourth of the Medical school was implicated, and surely there must have been good reasons to bury the case."

"You declared, several months ago, to a new female employee at the pharmacy, that a lover such as yourself had nothing at all in common with an ordinary lover and that any woman, after having known you, could not live without you."

Blushing slightly, Schuttringer tried to smile, but managed only a forced grimace.

"Madame Joly boasted that, thanks to you, she learned how to snort cocaine."

"There are thirty to forty thousand of us in Paris who snort ..."

"I'm only asking you to be accountable for your actions. Did you take care of one or several customers the night of the fourth to the fifth?"

"I filled two prescriptions."

"Did you set foot in the store itself?

"No!"

"So you didn't collect any money? And was Madame Joly responsible for all the figures recorded on the cash register?"

Schuttringer was quiet, stunned, suspicious, slightly worried.

"Thirteen sales yielded a grand total of ninety-six francs twenty-five. Two of those sales came from prescriptions that you filled. Ten others came from other sales. The thirteenth ..."

There was silence. Schuttringer did not move. His brow was wrinkled, his eyes were as prominent as ever. It seemed as though his attempts to understand were in vain.

"The thirteenth amount that was accounted for was the sum of five francs seventy-five. That amount, according to the pharmacist's formal testimony, could correspond only to a box of absorbent cotton B. No other product in that establishment, costs five francs seventy five."

Another silence. Monsieur Froget shuffled his papers. "Did you sell any absorbent cotton?"

"I didn't set foot into the store."

"Not a single box of cotton went off the shelves. It was easy to check on it since the night before a case had been opened and the boxes are still all accounted for."

"Which proves what exactly? ..."

"That there were five francs seventy-five too much in the register in the morning. Five francs seventy-five which were rung up by the register, which went into the cash drawer, but which represent no change in inventory whatsoever."

Schuttringer wiggled in his chair, but did not whisper a word.

Only after five minutes of silence did he get up lazily and ask without any particular firmness: "Well?"

✣ ✣ ✣

Monsieur Froget's voice was dry, and his attitude was so haughty, so scathing that the accused lost his assurance.

"The body could have gotten into the cellar only with your permission. Only one door, as you pointed out. By day, there were many people in the store who would have seen what was going on. At night, there were only you and Madame Joly, who was all yours in body and spirit. Therefore, you either committed the crime or were an accomplice. It's a rather strong presumption, in any case."

The rest of the reconstruction was brief. Monsieur Froget knew that the suspect was smart enough not to miss an iota of such extremely concentrated reasoning.

"On the fifth, Madame Joly waits for the arrival of the employees in order to leave. Let's still place this in the assumptions column. She is waiting merely because she needs to be seen. Or rather, you're the one who needs to have her seen. It would appear mathematically impossible to convict you, after that. The crime, however, has already been committed. The body is in the cellar, soaked in vitriol. That evening, the experts say that the death occurred to twenty-four hours earlier.

"Conclusion: the body is not that of Madame Joly.

"There are five francs seventy five too many in the cash register. Yet, neither you nor your mistress had anything to gain from putting money in it, from creating any kind of unnecessary irregularity.

"*A purchase was made. But what was bought was not taken out of the store.*

"We're talking about the absorbent cotton. A young woman comes in, receives the merchandise and pays. She is then led into the back of the store, killed, sliced up, stuffed down the cellar beneath the acid-soaked bags. Yet Madame Joly makes the mistake of putting the cotton back on the shelf, the very cotton that was purchased and that nonetheless did not leave the store because the person who bought it did not leave either. We might call this a mechanical proof."

In a vulgar gesture, Schuttringer put his hand on his bloated neck and said: "Another trophy in your collection! You're really proud of yourself, aren't you!"

But Monsieur Froget had already stopped listening, and was writing in his notebook: "Jealous, Joly becomes dangerous. Hard to kill him without taking any risks. And the lovers, for somewhat obscure reasons, need each other. Madame Joly was the one who would pretend to be dead. At night, when they are alone, they wait for someone to come in who more or less fits her description. Murder. A change of clothing. Vitriol. At eight o'clock, Madame Joly, *wearing a coat,* waits for the day workers to arrive, so that she can hide the dress that is not her own. She vanishes and waits for her lover at an agreed upon location."

I have read a little note that was later inserted between the lines in red ink: "Death at the Salpêtrière[1] old age home, of a general paralysis a year after having been acquitted for lack of criminal responsibility."

---

[1] The Salpêtrière home housed aged women, and also served as a mental institution for women.

The Seventh Culprit

WALDEMAR STRVZESKI

WALDEMAR STRVZESKI

"SIT DOWN!" said Monsieur Froget.

The first reaction of the accused was to laugh so much he bent over backwards, then, with a certain formality, he affected an artificial smile which suddenly made all his features seem pointy. He said: "Thank you! And I would like to tell you, *monsieur le juge*, what a relief it is for me to finally deal with a real man of the world."

Seating himself and making small hand gestures as he talked while Monsieur Froget watched him in as discouraging a manner as possible, he continued: "If I were still wearing my officer's uniform as a staff officer in the Polish army, the brutal behavior of your subordinates would be cause for diplomatic action. Having become a simple citizen and, moreover, a foreigner in this country, I am reduced to a position where I must suffer all this in silence."

He listened to himself speak with great satisfaction. He was a thin little man, dry, stiff as a stick. To his stupefaction, the jailor had watched him remove a corset, as he was undressing, worn by certain officers in the past. Waldemar had a chiseled face. He was very near-sighted and wore a golden pince-nez that he had to wipe off at every moment. To do this, he carried a piece of camel hair in the pocket of his waistcoat. He wore the correct clothes, with a knife-edge crease.

"Listen Strvzeski ..."

"Excuse-me ... *Strvzes* ... Do you understand? Look at my mouth ... *Strvzes* ... like this ... Then *ki* ... There are very few Frenchmen who can pronounce my name correctly and it's quite unpleasant ..."

Monsieur Froget did not flinch in the least. On the contrary! His coldness increased tenfold. "On Tuesday January 18th, you left your apartment on the rue Turenne, at eight o'clock in the morning."

"About that time, yes, *monsieur le juge*. I would like to point out to you, however ..."

"You bought a newspaper a hundred meters from there, at a draper's. She claims that your hand was trembling when you handed the five sous to her."

"I'm convinced that you are not considering the difference between a draper and a staff officer ..."

" ...Yet, you were able to read only one headline, written in bold lettering: *'Zirski and Protov were executed this morning ...'* "

"Every country has their rotten citizens, *monsieur le juge* ...And ..."

"You left the store in a rather agitated state. You walked all the way to the Place de la Republique and you entered a gunsmith's store. You asked for a revolver ..."

"An unloaded one, right?"

"Unloaded, indeed. The gunsmith was even surprised that you did not wish to supply yourself with bullets."

"You see ..."

"I see nothing. Before leaving, you went over to open the door. You became more and more nervous. You felt you needed to tell the merchant, who didn't ask any questions at all, that you were a staff officer ..."

"*Monsieur le juge*, I ..."

"You walked along the Grands Boulevards until you reached the Porte Saint-Denis. You turned at the corner of the rue Saint-Denis. The policeman you walked by mentioned that you were speaking volubly under your breath. He did not lose sight of you. You turned around three times. Then, suddenly, you entered a dairy shop. It was nine o'clock in the morning, a very bustling hour of the day in that neighborhood near the Halles ..."

Waldemar wiped his glasses off with care. Without these, his face was transformed. His eyes could no longer see. His eyelids were blinking as though they were in great pain.

"There was a female customer in the dairy shop. You took out your revolver from your pocket and you cried out: *'The cash register ... Quickly! ... Don't make any calls ...'* The customer ran out screaming. The policeman hurried over. The dairy shop owner fell to the floor behind her counter. You were met with no resistance. Is this an exact summary of what happened?"

"You must admit that it is painful for me to listen to ..."

"Very well! The Polish Embassy knows who you are. You claim to be a former staff officer without actually having been one. Before the war, you worked as a salesclerk in a Russian bookstore in Warsaw. When Poland was liberated, chance saw to it that you spoke French and that you should be attached to a staff-officer's division as an official interpreter. As such, you had the right to wear a uniform. It was a chaotic time. A newly independent Poland needed men. After a few months, you asked to be sent to Paris with the recently appointed military attaché. You were seen in the *Bois* riding a horse each morning. Then there was talk of having you switched to being a War Advisor, as you were taking advantage of your uniform to commit many petty acts of swindling. In order to avoid a scandal, they settled for your resignation."

"There's a lot to be said about that, *monsieur le juge*. But for that, a trial is needed, a *big* trial ..."

"You went back to being a salesclerk in a bookstore. Only this time, your specialty was in erotic works, special prints and even some photography."

"I would like to protest that a certain tolerance for ..."

"You moved into your apartment on the rue Turenne. Your room is on the third floor. A lady by the name of Boullant lives on the fourth, a sixty-five year old who had her moment of fame as a loose woman."

"The courteousness that we must show towards women should make you ..."

"Madame Boullant is fat and ugly, highly dropsical to boot. Rumor has it in the neighborhood that one of the Republic's most prominent figures, who had been her lover, gives her a stipend because of certain compromising letters. This did not escape your attention ..."

" I don't bother with *ragots*[1] ... (is this the right word in French?) ... staircase *ragots* ..."

"But you became Madame Boullant's lover."

Waldemar managed a smile that was at once discrete and accusatory.

"You would go up to her room almost every night. The neighbors on your floor enjoyed listening to the arguments that would break out between you two."

The Pole assumed an increasingly offended posture and murmured:

"I am shocked, *monsieur le juge*, that a man as worldly as yourself would ..."

The next question was completely unexpected: "What relationship did you have with the two murderers who were executed on the 8th of January?"

---

[1] Gossip

"But ... I ... don't see ..."

"Just a minute. Zirski, Protov, as well as three accomplices who were sentenced to forced labor, broke into the Polish Embassy on the night of November 24th to the 25th, and caught in the act of their burglary, savagely killed two guards. A preliminary investigation determined that this was not a trial run for them. They were found guilty of two other murders perpetrated in the Seine *département*, committed in isolated houses. Protov admitted that, on Saturday the 21st of November, he was ready to break into the Embassy, but the fortuitous presence of two agents on the street forced him to delay the burglary until the 24th. He swore under oath that he did not expect that the premises would be guarded and that the double murder was therefore not premedidated. On the 21st, however, the Embassy was unguarded."

"I don't suppose you're going to accuse me of ..."

"I know that yours were not among the many fingerprints found on the premises."

"You see that? ..."

"On the other hand, you were seen having an aperitif on several occasions at the Saint-Antoine Bar, on the corner of the rue de Turenne and the rue Saint-Antoine, which the Polish gang used as their headquarters."

"I believe, *monsieur le juge*, that if one sought out all the places where you drank aperitifs, one would discover that ..."

And it was Waldemar's turn to wipe his glasses once again.

"Do you admit that since the bandits' arrest, you have not set foot in that bar?"

"You see! As soon as I found out that it was a sleazy establishment, I ..."

"What sum of money did you hope to steal in the dairy shop on the rue Saint-Denis?"

Silence. Or rather, Waldemar muttered to himself in a hushed voice.

"On that particular morning, there were two hundred francs in your wallet. Madame Boullant's neighbors state that there haven't been any scenes between you two for several days now."

Waldemar looked worriedly at the judge, searching for the hidden meaning in that sentence.

"In other words, several days have gone by *without your asking her for any money*."

He became agitated. His indignation was such that he jumped up in one motion and, gesticulating, began: "*Monsieur le juge*, you forget ..."

"Be seated!"

It was an order. The man let himself fall to his seat as he grumbled: "You must admit that for a well-mannered man who has known the situation that you ..."

"Why did you need money on the morning of the 18th?"

Silence. Monsieur Froget himself was quiet. Waldemar ended the silence by saying: "I demand to be examined by a psychiatric doctor. There is no doubt that, since my misfortunes, I am no longer the same man. A change has taken place in my brain."

"In the Polish expatriate community near the place Saint-Paul, you were known as 'the lawyer.'"

"Because of my training ...."

"Or because of your obsessive need to give advice. This is why you wrote up a flowery advertisement for a tailor on the rue des Francs-Bourgeois, which he did not dare print in the newspapers ... On the rue de Turenne, you claimed you were connecting your room to Madame Boullant's by what you called a country telephone. You fashioned a hole in the ceiling, bought some batteries and some wire. The telephone never worked ..."

"For completely accidental reasons. Surely you are familiar with the principle of ..."

"You promised the concierge that you would find her son a job as pilot for an airline responsible for the Central European routes. In truth, your role was limited to your giving the address of a flight school."

"I don't see the link between ..."

"Madame Boullant claims that, on several occasions, you entered her apartment while she was gone."

"Did I take anything?"

"You were looking for some letters. How much did you earn from trading in pornography?"

"Around two thousand francs per month ..."

"Which, in addition to the generous contributions from your mistress, comes to almost three thousand francs. You are not known for any vice in particular."

Waldemar grinned from ear to ear, and nodded with an obvious sense of self-satisfaction.

"No doubt, you did not have enough time to read the newspaper you purchased on the 18th of January at the draper's. It relates that when they came to wake them up to announce that they would be executed, Zirski and Protov reacted in different ways. Protov clenched his fists, became pale and, up until the very last minute, spouted threats in Polish. As for Zirski, he tapped the prison warden in the stomach and burst out laughing. With a strong accent, he shouted: " — *You old trickster!"*

Waldemar wiped his glasses. His nostrils were pinched, he was short of breath.

"On the other hand, at the moment he was pushed towards the guillotine, he fainted ...."

"What can I ... I ..."

"Where were you on the night of the 24th to 25th of November?"

"In Bordeaux, on business."

"Would you please give us the list of clients that you had seen?"

"I saw no one. They were gone. But I occupied room 78 at the Hotel de la Marine. I signed a register, which should be enough to prove where I was."

"On what day did you leave Paris?"

"On the 21st, around noon."

"On Saturday then. With a round trip ticket, of course."

"Yes. I'm very tired. I would like to add that I do not feel very well ...."

"Your head hurts?"

"That's right ... like a whirlpool ... or rather like waves that come and go, that knock a little bone somewhere in your body ... For God's sake, why did I attack that dairy shopkeeper? ..."

"I will tell you!" Monsieur Froget answered. He had been writing for some time now in his notebook.

✣ ✣ ✣

"I am waiting for you to give me the honor of ..."

But Monsieur Froget said nothing, continued to write. When he was finished, he pushed his open notebook towards the accused who read the following with displeasure:

"Had attacked the dairy shopkeeper because he considered going to prison, and, preferably a mental institution (his unexplainable act should put him in the latter) as the best way to escape the wrath of the Polish bandits.

"A very inconsistent creature, inferior to all the positions he had previously occupied but judged them to be beneath him. His rank in the army went to his head. Complications when dealing with the diplomatic world.

"Becomes Madame Boullant's lover because she possesses some documents that can be used against a very important person. From then on, brags about being all powerful. Pontificates, doles out advice left and right. Needs to show off, and especially to feel his superiority.

"At the Saint-Antoine Bar, meets the Polish gang. He gives them advice, just as he had done for the tailor. Mentions a *coup* against the embassy, against which he holds a grudge. Masterminds the expedition which must take place on a Saturday, the only day that the embassy is not guarded.

"*And so he leaves for Bordeaux on Saturday* (even though no business is ever conducted on Sunday) *in order to create an alibi for himself.* Because of a fortuitous accident, his accomplices hit the embassy three days later. A bunch of unpolished ruffians. Didn't realize that the plan no longer worked. Five out of seven are arrested, after the guards' murder.

"Waldemar comes back to Paris. Continues to show off. Promises the remaining bandits that they will not be arrested, thanks to the Boullant's documents, which he doesn't even have in his possession. They threaten to kill him if the arrested accomplices are executed.

"He stalls for time, lives on a day to day basis. He no longer even tries to find the Boullant papers. Is aware of his impotence. Learns of the execution. Feels as though he is being followed. Doesn't have time to flee and commits an unbelievable act in order to place himself under police protection."

And underneath, the Pole read:

"*Proof* — Takes off for Bordeaux on Saturday. Returns the day after the incident.

"*Assumptions* — Chooses a store with two people in it (so that one of them can pull the alarm.)

"The weapon is not loaded.

"Doesn't need the money and cannot hope to find a large sum at nine o'clock in the morning in a dairy shop.

"No longer frequents the Saint-Antoine Bar."

Finally, written in the margin: "Crushed by the role he wanted to play."

Waldemar Strvzeski put his pince-nez back on, and said convulsively: "For a man who had been ..."

"A staff officer, yes ..."

And the Pole said in a strangled voice: "It's hard!"

The Eighth Culprit

PHILIPPE

PHILIPPE

POLICE INSPECTOR LUCAS of the P.J.,[1] who had been put in charge of the preliminary investigation, had notified the Judge. "You'll tell me what effect this has on you ... It's hard to know ... It's not the same being in there."

And Monsieur Froget was "in there," that is to say in a strange lodging on the rue Bréa. Most of the tenants lived with their doors and windows open. Few of the window panes had been washed. The ones in 7 *bis* had no doubt never been washed.

Monsieur Froget had knocked, as there was no doorbell. Philippe, wearing a blue smock, just like the ones that had been described to the judge, had opened the door before fading away with a worrisome little laugh.

A Bedroom? A Dining room? A Kitchen? It was all of that, and it was something undefinable as well. Old carpets everywhere, pieces of discolored material, spread out along the walls. There were carpets still on the tables, sloppily drooping from armchairs. A profusion of somber tatters the aim of which was no doubt to give some semblance of comfort.

"*Monsieur le juge*, I presume? ... Please sit down ..."

After having observed him for a few seconds, Monsieur Froget noted that there were two aspects to him, because of the asymmetry of his face. If one looked at him at a profile, he was a young man who

---

[1] *Palais Justice*, the headquarters of the French equivalent of the British Criminal Investigation Department.

seemed sweet and tender; the contrast between his clear blue eyes and his dark hair gave him a certain charm that was too pronounced not to be annoying. But if one looked at him face to face, one noticed that his nose was quite long, twisted, and that his mouth had an abnormal curl to it.

He wore a woman's smock. His mannerisms were all feminine — his way of doing household chores, how he wiped his hands, and the way that he bowed his head as he waited for his visitor to speak.

And so Monsieur Froget watched the single bed, the laundry which was drying, the portrait of two men in a golden frame, and he understood the importance of Lucas's words. He should have known and expected all this. He felt that he was suddenly cast into a world that was fundamentally counterfeit.

"I do not believe you knew your mother, did you?"

"Nor my father. I am a natural child and my parents had the good sense to get rid of me. I was raised by peasants, near Turin, then sent to a juvenile detention center ..."

"When you were twenty-one years old, you were hired as a valet. You had several positions. You came to France along with your next to last employers. When you were with the last ones, you met Forestier who was a maitre d'."

"Yes, *monsieur le juge*. It was Monsieur Forestier who took care of me ..."

Forestier's portrait was was there. A man in his fifties, big, thin, with withered features, deathly pale skin, flabby legs and an uncertain gait caused by his rheumatism. His clothes and hair were gray.

Eight hours earlier, in a hotel room on the rue des Batignolles, where he was found with a woman who was registered with the Vice Squad, Forestier suddenly became delirious, his eyeballs had become so big that the women was sick with horror. One hour later, he died at Beaujon without ever having regained consciousness. The autopsy revealed that the death was due to an absorption of a strong dose of atropine. In the pockets of the deceased, in addition to a certain number of letters, three thousand francs were found as well as a small cardboard box which still contained two pills. The latter were filled with a small amount of digitalin, which was not enough to cause any problems, and a massive amount of atropine.

The Berthomieu girl, Forestier's occasional companion, declared: "He accosted me behind the Gaumont Palace movie theater. I knew him, as he came over from time to time. He made us believe that he lived in the provinces and that he spent eight to ten days a month in Paris. He chose one or two women each time. He was quite generous. Sometimes, he would go on a binge and keep us for several days at a time. He took three pills from his box right after dinner, even though I laughed and asked him if he needed a boost ..."

The first report, which was signed by the neighborhood police commissioner, concluded that Forrestier had committed suicide.

No sooner had Police Inspector Lucas become in charge of the case then it yielded one surprise after another.

"Forestier, Jules-Raymond-Claude," read Froget who had summarized his notes himself in his little notebook. "Born at Saint-Amand-Montrond. Expelled from that town's high school, one year before graduating, right after a dormitory scandal. Employed in Paris. And then he became the personal secretary for the Count of B ..., who had a champion of legitimism.[2] Fired for unknown reasons. Maitre d' in Monte-Carlo, then Nice. Meets Philippe and moves to Paris with

---

[2] A royalist movement

him. They live off their swindling."

But with such an individual, one cannot speak of a banal form of swindling. Forestier had become, as he was later to be called, *the Bourbon family swindler*.

The letters that were found on him, then at the rue Bréa, were very informative in regards to his methodology. He would write to old men who were smitten with the idea of nobility and lost in provincial gentility, would pass himself off as a Bourbon agent, or as a persecuted legitimist or even as a propagandist whose job it was to raise the necessary funds for the creation of a new royalist newspaper. On occasion, he would show up in person. Some would be suspicious of him. Others, most in fact, would be sparing in their praise. But some others, the more naive ones, fell hook, line and sinker.

Lucas had noted in his report: "A firm believer in homeopathic remedies, Forestier bought all his medicine from a pharmacy on the boulevard Bonne-Nouvelle where, for the last few weeks, they practically administered minimal daily doses of pure atropine as is the habit of such dispensaries."

Philippe, who had taken his smock off and put on a jacket instead — dressed like that he resembled a transvestite! — waited for questions from the magistrate with a vague smile on his lips.

"Oh! I ..." He said this softly, with resignation. "I was doing the housework, wasn't I? It's an incredible amount of work! And the laundry! And the ironing! And everything ..."

It took a considerable amount of willpower not to slap him across the face.

"Then, Monsieur Forestier had me write letters. Sometimes a few hundred copies of the same one ... Then, I put stamps on the envelopes ... He was almost always waiting outside ... He traveled to the provinces often ..."

"Or in and around the Gaumont Palace in Paris!"

Philippe's face suddenly puckered up for a second. But Monsieur Froget hardly noticed as a smile returned to his face.

"I don't understand!" he said with an exasperating sweetness. "There's a mystery in all this ... Here! Here's a post-card from Luchon that I received two days after his death ... the postmark is on it ... It's is handwriting all right ... Here's another one which came today ... Why don't you interrogate the concierge and the postman ..."

The judge nervously picked up the two cards. Philippe was telling the truth. The postmarks were authentic. The handwriting, if it had been forged, had been forged by a specialist who was much more accomplished than Philippe was.

"It's like the three thousand francs," continued the latter, nodding his head. "We never had that kind of money. Here! Here are the socks that I had to darn over twenty times ... In the evening, we ate only vegetable soup and some cream cheese ... The concierge will back me up, as will the food-sellers. I had ten dollars per day for food ... And Monsieur Forestier always needed medicine ..."

"Is he sick?"

"He had difficulty breathing sometimes. But I think he read his medical book too often. He took a ton of drugs."

"Atropine?"

"I never heard him utter that word. I know his pills, in the cardboard box, contained some digitalin for his shortness of breath."

"When he went away on trips, did he always send you postcards?"

"Almost every day."

"Did he often go to Luchon?"

"Every month, or every other month. He had 'clients' there ..."
And Philippe smiled as if to make excuses for using that word. "Do
you mean that I am one of his 'clients' as well?"

"Did you know him to have a mistress?"

"Oh! *Monsieur le juge* ..."

Monsieur Froget turned his head despite himself, feeling the need
to look outside where the sun was really shining.

"Is it true that, at the juvenile detention center, you were being
treated for mental problems, and then excused from military service
for the same reason?"

"I had a few lapses ... it still happens to me from time to time, but
much more rarely ... as though I had difficulty thinking ... then
everything gets completely mixed up ..."

"Did Monsieur Forestier ever beat you?"

"No! He was a good master ..." (the word gave the judge a start) "...
he was just a little stingy ... Here! These clothes were tailored from
one of his old suits ... It's like his shirts that I have to wear, even
though they are too big ..."

"What were you doing on the day he died?"

"He left at four o'clock, he told me he was going to take the train
to Luchon and that he would be gone for eight days. He left me some
letters to copy. I straightened up his room, then I went over to chat
with the concierge. When she went to bed, I went home ..."

"During the course of the evening, you asked that woman if your
eyes weren't getting bigger and she made fun of you. Shortly after you
left, she heard your footsteps in the courtyard."

"To empty out the garbage in the garbage can."

"That's exactly right. Normally, you do this right after dinner.
And you rarely entered the lodge."

Philippe

"It was an idea that came to me all of a sudden ..."

"A little later, the concierge was awakened by the cats who were fighting. She looked out the window and she saw them eating. By the gaslight, she noticed, among other things, a big piece of Swiss cheese. In the morning, a dead cat was lying in the courtyard and his eyes were bulging from his head."

"I don't know anything about that."

"Why had you thrown out that cheese?"

"It was spoiled."

"And yet you bought your supplies on a daily basis, in small quantities. Where did Monsieur Forestier put all his medicine?"

"In this closet over here."

Monsieur Froget opened it. It also functioned as a pantry. There was some leftover ragout stuck to a plate, some powdered sugar on a plate, a half a stick of margarine.

On the highest shelf, there was a homeopathic medical book and a few flasks with the Boulevard Bonne-Nouvelle address written on them. They were excessively small flasks, in brown glass, that are only used in homeopathic pharmacies that sell pure poison, but in infinitely small quantities.

Each of the bottles would fit in the palm of a hand. They contained a variety of medicines, the names of which were written on the label, and which confirmed Monsieur Forestier's obsession with drugs. But the ones that contained the atropine — and there should have been about twenty of them, according to the pharmacist — were no longer there.

"Did you throw away the empty bottles?"

"No. But three days before Monsieur Forestier's death, the concierge pointed out to me that he must have been quite sick, because she saw little flasks in the wastebasket every day."

Monsieur Froget grabbed a flask that was bigger than the rest of them, the only one without a label. He uncorked it, sniffed it, did not hesitate to wet the tip of his tongue. It was water!

"Who filled up this bottle?"

"Monsieur Forestier."

"With water?"

"I don't know. He poured the contents of the brown flasks into the bottle, then threw them away."

"And you didn't know what he was going to do with them?"

"That's right ... I don't know anything."

"When did you buy the Swiss cheese?"

"Wait ... it was in the evening ... yes, the night before Monsieur Forestier's trip ..."

Monsieur Froget opened the door, and simply told the inspector who had remained in the courtyard: "To the Dépôt!"[3]

And he pointed to Philippe who had burst into tears.

✠ ✠ ✠

Beneath a title, *"The Forestier Case,"* Monsieur Froget's notebook reads:

"Proof of Philippe's guilt — *presence of pure water in the flask where atropine had accumulated.*

"Forestier, who was already dying from the atropine, had in fact been trying to poison his companion as well. But if he also had poisoned himself, he would not have needed to set up the situaion with the flasks and the water bottle.

"1. Philippe had spent the evening at the concierge's, which he

---

[3]A holding cell for prisoners awaiting execution.

rarely did.

"2. He asked her if his eyes had gotten bigger, the first symptom of atrophine poisoning.

"3. He had carelessly thrown the cheese away. *Which meant that he was frightened, but he did not know for sure whether the cheese was poisoned or not.*

"Recapping all the facts: Forestier, a vicious maniac, latches on to the degenerate Philippe, at the start of his swindling, even though they do not bring in very much money. Treats the young man like a slave. As soon as he has some money, he goes out and spends it.

"But Philippe is jealous. Forrestier therefore has a cohort send cards from the provinces whenever he is in Paris with his mistrress. But he finds this situation with Philippe to be a burden so he stocks up on atropine.

"Philippe, who senses his companion's discontent with him, watches over the medicine. On the day of Forestier's departure, he notices that the level of liquid that had accumulated in a bottle had gone down.

"He mixes the remaining atropine with the digitalin in the pills that Forestier takes him. This is his revenge. Once Forestier has left, Philippe avoids touching any food in the house. And, in order to avoid being accused of murder, he fills the flask with pure water."

That's all. Or rather, there is a word in the margins. And Monsieur Froget must have been painfully impressed to have used a word so foreign to his measured vocabulary:

"Sinister!"

The Ninth Culprit

NICOLAS

NICOLAS

THE CONTRAST between Monsieur Froget and Nicolas was striking. Froget would not make even the slightest concession in adapting to the milieu, and Nicolas who felt at home as soon as he walked through the door.

And yet, thanks to his personal prestige, Monsieur Froget was not ridiculous. Even though he was dressed in black from head to toe, as was his custom, he was not in evening dress.

Although he was not familiar with *Picratt's*, he was at ease, as he brusquely entered the cabaret's frenzy, brushing against some obsequious boys and scantily clad women with sharp laughs. Nicolas was wearing a smoking jacket. With the ease of a man of the world, with only the tiniest touch of humility, he led the judge to the second floor and opened the door to a private sitting room.

"Is it here?"

"It's here ..."

Nicolas closed the door behind him and waited. He was about fifty-years old, but with a closely shaven face, a healthy complexion, a relatively clear eye, he had a cheeful contenance. Without being fat, he had a certain stockiness that gave him a *bon vivant*'s figure that took nothing away from his distinguished appearance. His smile betrayed the kind of melancholic toleration of those who have seen much of life and who no longer have any great expectations. He was Russian from head to toe and even up to the tips of his fingernails, with, occasionally and fleetingly, the airs of a great lord. In his hand, he held an intricate and ornate cigarette case which he held hesitatingly. He finally said:

"Excuse me, *Monsieur* ... But it is very painful for me to stay here and not smoke and, if you don't mind ..."

Froget acquiesced by quivering his eyelids, and leaned against the fireplace on which he placed his bowler hat. "Did you know William Haynes before he left Paris last week?"

"Not even by name. He used a messenger at his hotel to send me a card telling me that a friend of Assatourof would be happy to see me. Assatourof is a compatriot I had lost sight of for fifteen years and who had moved to Oakland. Haynes, he told me, owns an air-pump factory in that city."

"He showed himself quite cordial to you right from the start, he invited you to his table ..."

There was a delicate smile from Nicolas as he took small puffs from his cigarette with cardboard edges. "Very cordial, yes, at his table. Like an American who's worth a million dollars."

"He asked you to accompany him through Paris at night."

"That's right. First we went to a music-hall, then to a cabaret which Haynes loudly proclaimed to be lugubrious. He wanted women. I took him to a *brasserie* on the avenue Montaigne where ..."

"... Where you introduced him to two women you knew."

Nicolas volunteered calmly: "Two women who had long lived in the same hotel as I did, at a time when life was much more painful for me than it is now. We used to dine at the same restaurant. They were good friends of mine."

"The four of you then continued the rounds of the cabarets. You went into three establishments and Haynes did not seem any more enthusiastic. One question. Who payed?"

"Me! From my companion's account, naturally. At diner, he declared to me that Paris was a cut-throat for foreigners in general, and for Americans in particular, and he had no intention of being robbed. He handed me three thousand francs ..."

"Which he took from his wallet?"

"Yes. He begged me to pay for him."

"Did he carry any other bills in the wallet?

"Certainly. Haynes had asked for change for a thousand dollars in front of me at the hotel front desk."

"Did you take taxis?"

"Of course not! He arrived from Europe with his valet who doubles as his chauffeur. His first order of business was to rent a Chrysler for a month."

"After a long discussion among themselves, your companions admitted that you had had a lot to drink and that you seemed nervous."

From Nicolas: silence.

"Haynes even criticized you for it."

"I don't deny it. Let us say that ..."

"Well?"

"It's a very tricky thing to express. Let us say, if you like, that I thought him a bit too American. With the others and with myself!"

"Was it your idea to dine in a private suite rather than at a cabaret? Why?"

"For the reason I just gave you. In another establishment, where I am very well known and where I have several friends in the balalaika orchestra, I had barely escaped embarrassment when Haynes interrupted a Russian melody by demanding some jazz ... Moreover, I will admit to you that I was counting on slipping away without any explanations."

"When they got to *Picratt's*, the two women went towards the restroom."

"That's what they usually do. They were freshening up."

"You remained alone in the sitting room with Haynes. That's when a boy who happened to be in the staircase heard the glass shattering and a cry. When he arrived in the hallway, you were at the door. Haynes tried to sit up. Lying on the rug, he was losing great amounts of blood from a ten centimeter bruise on his scalp and another wound was later to be found on his right wrist. Your companions returned and there was a moment of chaos. When Haynes could finally speak, he accused you of having attacked him for his wallet. He no longer had it in his pocket."

"The wallet was no more in mine than his. An officer had searched me before I could leave the room."

"What do you have to say for yourself?"

"Nothing, monsieur."

He did not say *monsieur le juge* like most of the accused. There was a undercurrent that one found in all of the Russian's positions.

"What was your profession before the war?"

"Captain in a regiment that was garrisoned in Odessa. I had a small income. Life was easy."

"Witnesses say that you were very recognized in the most exclusive circles and that, during the season in Yalta, you were considered the don Juan of the seaside resort."

"I was a bachelor. As I said, life was easy."

"What have you been you living on since the revolution?"

A short moment of silence. Nicolas folded the tip of his cigarette into small pieces. "You must have learned that as well. Subsidies which come to me from various sources here and there. I have only a few needs!"

Nicolas

He noticed the judge's staring at his smoking jacket, which was cut to perfection, and at his impeccably tailored shirt. He added with a tinge of reproach in his voice: "One can wear evening dress every night, frequent elegant surroundings and spend so little."

Froget knew that it was Nicolas's room, on the rue de la Montagne-Sainte-Geneviève, rented for two hundred francs a month. It was a tiny closet without any air.

Every so often, the Russian did not leave the room for three or four days, smoking cigarettes, drinking tea and eating God knows what.

"You have numerous associations, not only in the expatriate community in Paris, but in French society. Each summer you are invited to some villa on the coast of Normandie. Each fall, you would hunt in someone's chateau or another."

Nicolas began to pace up and down the room noiselessly, with an agility that clashed with his stockiness. At certain times, he seemed like a philosopher on whom life smiled all the time, who smiles at everything, because of everything.

Then, suddenly, he seemed to shrink, to age: one could notice some sagging flesh, the weariness in his blue eyes and a slight trembling at the corner of his lips.

"I did not steal!" he pronounced brusquely, as an answer to his own thoughts rather than to Froget's questions. And once again, he covered the room from one end to the other, three times over, continued in another tone of voice: "Some options are physically impossible. Only one door, which opens onto the hallway. The window was and has remained closed. It's been proved. I suppose that they searched under the rug and behind the furniture. I notice traces of dust which show that the mirror was removed. And yet, I was searched before leaving that room."

"You forget that Haynes had been there as well, at his formal request."

"I know!"

"We thought for a moment that you had passed the wallet on to one of your female companions or to a boy. But the officer had examined everything that was in the sitting room."

"You see?"

"Excuse me! I don't see anything! You admit that you had struck Haynes on the head with a bottle of champagne. You could have killed him. He's got to spend two more weeks in bed and he'll probably have to wear a wig."

Nicolas could not suppress a satisfied smile.

"What happened between you two?"

"Nothing! Let us suppose that I had over-indulged. I had been drinking. I was nervous. Drunkenness makes me into a misanthrope and encourages me to become indignant at things that should perhaps make me smile."

"Did he say something to you?"

"What difference does it make why I hit him. I didn't steal anything."

"Basically, you take responsibility only for striking and wounding him."

"Yes."

"And yet, Haynes himself formally accuses you of violent theft, even attempted murder."

Nicolas shrugged his shoulders.

"Did you have money troubles?"

"As soon as I was old enough to think logically. It all began when I was nine years old, I believe, when I started borrowing from my

French teacher."

"Did you and Haynes agree on the amount of money you would give the two women?"

A moment of hesitation.

"No ..."

"This afternoon, Haynes claimed that you had come up with the sum of five hundred francs for each of them."

"That's possible. I would add, that's the normal price."

"At what time did you put this amount into words?"

"I don't remember anymore."

"Did you speak English?"

"No. Russian, French and German."

"Does Haynes know two of these languages?"

"Only one: French"

"From the moment you met them in the *brasserie* until the moment you came here, were you — you and Haynes — ever separated from your female companions for one second ?"

"No."

"If my reports are accurate, they weren't professionals so to speak. At least they did not identify themselves as such when they signed the police registry."

"Your reports are correct. One of them was married to an industrialist from the North."

"When you entered *Picratt's,* how much was left of the three thousand francs Haynes gave you?"

"About half."

"You did not ask him for any money?"

"No, sir."

Each time that there was a moment of silence, one could hear echoes of jazz and the swell of dance steps from the dance hall.

"Let's leave!" said Monsieur Froget suddenly as he walked towards the door.

Thanks to the intervention of a political figure, Nicolas had been set free on probation.

The two men soon found themselves on the street corner. But the judge let three empty taxis pass by without hailing them.

"Let's walk! ..."

It was chilly outdoors. The rue Notre-Dame-de-Lorette was deserted. Nicolas mechanically handed his cigarette case to Monsieur Froget who refused it with a hand gesture.

"Of course, I'm indicting you for the blows and the wounds, and ..."

"And ... ?"

They walked for ten steps in silence.

"Officially, that's all! ...But, between you and me ..."

Nicolas lowered his head. Ten more steps.

"Yes it's wretched ..." he said as he looked elsewhere.

✛ ✛ ✛

"What insult did he hurl at you?"

"His whole attitude, first of all ... He pretended to treat me like a servant ... he would use hurtful words to ask questions about my life, then spoke about his millions immediately afterwards. Somewhere, as I was giving a hundred francs tip to the waiter — we drank eight hundred francs worth of champagne! — he took the bill back from his hands, handed it to me and said: ' — take half of this, please!' It doesn't matter. At *Picratt's*, I told him that I would leave him before the end of the evening and I advised him to hand over five hundred francs to each of the women. He laughed. He acted as though five hundred dollars were more than enough. I insisted. I was nervous. And so he declared that ..." Nicolas had trouble saying it. "... that I was defending my cut, even that the two women worked for me. I hit him. Automatically! The bottle shattered on his head and he collapsed."

"And so you leaned over him," Monsieur Froget continued. "You were suddenly tempted to seize his wallet. You held his arm. You had no other reason to hold his arm, as he was on the floor and unarmed ..."

"I did it out of rage more than the desire for money. I think that I would have given it to the two women ..."

"That's very likely. You didn't have to give it to them, *because Haynes did not have his wallet on him*. This same man who begged you to pay for him for fear that he would be robbed was not about to keep twenty thousand francs or a bit more in his pocket for a night of drunkenness. He had no doubt handed them over to his chauffeur ... But your gesture gave him the idea for revenge ... To have you found guilty for robbery and attempted murder ... which brought the case to another level ..."

And Froget said goodbye with a brusk flick of his hat, got into a car while Nicolas stood disconcerted in the middle of the sidewalk.

At three o'clock in the morning, the judge, who was at home, scribbled in his notebook:

"1. Nicolas did not steal, since he could not have hidden the wallet in the room in the presence of Haynes who did not lose consciousness. And Haynes could not have hidden it in Nicolas's presence. Therefore, there was no wallet. Consequently, Haynes knew that he was lying. But Nicolas could not reveal the wallet's absence without admitting that he had gone through his companion's pockets.

"2. If Nicolas had attacked his companion with the intent to rob him, he would have chosen a little less noisy weapon than a bottle; he could have used one of the andirons, for example. He struck in a fit of passion. Given the relationship between the two men, this could only have occurred on the heels of an insulting remark;

"3. Only one lie during the interrogation. First, he denies that this had anything to do with retribution on behalf of the women. Then he admits to it, without saying when the conversation took place. Yet, the two men had only been in the *Picratt's* sitting room.

"In short: an insulting remark during the course of a discussion about the women; blow; attempted robbery."

And Monsieur Froget went to bed.

The Tenth Culprit

THE TIMMERMANS

THE TIMMERMANS

THE FACTS were rather muddled, the witnesses were tentative or contradictory, what was certain and uncertain was so poorly delineated that Monsieur Froget was forced to fall back on a classic procedure of establishing an objective summary of all the pertinent information.

Here is the state of the summary at the moment that, in the magistrate's office, the formal questioning of the Timmermans couple was underway.

"On February 3, the Powell Circus opened in Nogent-sur-Marne after a series of short jumps from Brussels. The tent was set up on the Place de Paris. Some of the performers live in the caravans. Others stay at the Gambetta Hotel. (Note: 3rd class hotel. At night, the door is closed, but the guests can open it from the inside. To get in, they have to ring and call out their number as they pass by the porter's wicket.)

"The Timmermans, who make up an acrobatic bicycle act with their niece, Henny, occupy rooms 15 and 16 on the third floor of the hotel. They've been a part of the Powell Circus for five months. Joined when the circus was passing through Antwerp. At that time, had just finished a disastrous run in South America.

"Jack Lieb, thirty-two years old, bachelor, juggler having signed a one-month contract with Powell, occupies room 6, on the second floor.

"Performances continued until February 17. Jack Lieb, a handsome young man, flirts with most of the women and Henny in particular.

"The 18th, an open day. Departure for La Varenne is set for the 19th. Jack Lieb and Henny are seen at eight o'clock taking the tramway for Paris, without any luggage, Henny tells someone that they're going to the movies.

"At half past midnight, the hotel porter, who had already gone to bed, opens the door and hears a guest cry out No. 6. He is pretty sure that it is Lieb's voice. But he didn't know him well and can't be positive. Nor is he sure whether he heard one or two people come in.

"The Timmermans spent the evening in a café in Nogent, came home at ten o'clock.

"At three in the morning, the porter confusedly hears footsteps of people leaving the hotel. Thinks there were several people.

"*He doesn't open the door again that night.* At eight o'clock, the Timmermans make a ruckus and announce that their niece has run away. Say that they haven't seen her since the night before at seven o'clock. Her bed in room 16 is untouched. Her bags have disappeared.

"They point the finger at Jack Lieb. Knock on his door. No answer. *Lieb has disappeared, along with his trunk.*

"The rest of the company react to the news with cynicism. The circus leaves Nogent. On the 19th, it opens at La Varenne. Lieb's act is replaced. Without Henny, the Timmermans shorten their act, place an ad for a new partner in the trade papers.

"On February 23, the barge *Deux-Frères*, attempting to moor a hundred meters upstream from the Nogent bridge, strikes the bottom, in spite of the fact that its draft is less than normal depth. The bargeman starts probing with the help of a boat hook, brushes against an obstruction, alerts the lock keeper. After another probe, a trunk with the initials J.L. is removed from the water. When they open the trunk, they find Jack Lieb's corpse. The murderer must have bent him in half. Soggy bank notes (three hundred franc notes and five packs of ten) are floating around the corpse, wallet intact in his pocket. The autopsy reveals that Jack Lieb had been strangled and that the crime took place around the 18th.

"The spot where the trunk was fished out is nine hundred meters away from the Gambetta Hotel. Dry, the trunk and the body weigh 228 pounds. Hanny's body is searched for in vain. She is not found dead or alive, and as of February 25th, there has been no sign of her.

"The Powell Circus performers accuse the Timmermans of the murder, but have no proof. The couple always had a bad reputation and, wherever they've been, small objects, wallets, purses have disappeared without their being caught in the act."

✢ ✢ ✢

Facing Froget: a fifty-year old man and a forty-eight year old woman.

Frantz Timmermans was born in Workum, northern Netherlands. But he spent most of his youth in Belgium. At twenty, he joined a large German circus as a stable hand. At thirty, he marries Célina Vandeven, a tightrope walker from Ghent. Célina looks after her dead sister's daughter. The child is dragged all over Europe. Soon, the Timmermans trio is performing their bicycle act which has only moderate success. And from then on, year follows year without change. They go from one circus to another, perform in country fairs and, from time to time, in provincial music-halls.

Frantz is fed up. Everything has hardened in him: his skin, the lines of his hand, the stubborn expression of his sharply drawn features.

On Froget's desk, there is a photo of him performing his act; he is semi-acrobatic; semi-clown-like.   In the same photo, Célina Timmermans is standing on the shoulders of her husband who is riding a bicycle.

"To be blunt, Timmermans," says Monsieur Froget who is looking elsewhere, "your act has been unsuccessful for ten years."

The woman's bosom rises. She is about to speak. But the judge does not hear her.

"In your former engagements, as in your contract with Powell, you were specifically instructed to join the clowns in running onto the stage during the intermission for the whole evening. *Madame*, moreover, acted as the stable girls's dresser."

Timmermans said nothing. His dark grey eyes have a hard glint.

"Furthermore, your act was often canceled for one reason or the other. You were booed in Nogent ..."

Madame Timmermans becomes agitated, leans over, gesticulates, her mouth wide open.

"You had the poorest billing in the whole troop. You complained to whoever would listen. You've been complaining for ten years ..."

Timmermans sneaks a side glance at the judge. His jaws begin to sag.

"It has been established that, you have committed numerous petty thefts at the expense of your comrades."

"That's not true! They want to sink us ... they ..."

Suddenly, it is Madame Timmermans who gets up and speaks.

"Please be seated, madame. And only answer my questions. The end of your act consists, if I understand it correctly, of a tour of the ring, on a bicycle, your husband carrying you on his shoulders, while your niece stands on yours ..."

"Yes ... And we are the only ones who ..."

"Henny is twenty-two years old now, isn't she?"

"Was!" corrected Madame Timmermans.

"If you wish. It has been established that she had taken on quite a few lovers, with your blessing."

The man is quiet. The woman becomes indignant.

"Is it our fault that she was a loose woman?"

"Did you know that she was going to Paris with Lieb on the 18th?"

"We thought as much ..."

"You saw her as she was leaving. She had no luggage. Then she came back in the middle of the night. Your rooms were next to each other ... you did not hear a thing."

"Nothing ... except ..."

It appears that Madame Timmermans is afraid of letting her husband speak. She answers the questions quickly.

"Would you like to tell me exactly what your belongings consist of?"

"First there are our cycles and our gear, which remain with the circus and travel in the wagons. Then we have a wicker trunk and a black wooden chest, for clothes and the rest. Finally two little suitcases, one for Henny, the other one for ourselves."

"Were the two trunks in your room?"

"Yes!"

"Was your niece's suitcase in hers?"

"Yes ... she took it away with her ..."

"With everything in it? ..."

"Everything ... except for her stage clothes, which are always at the circus ..."

"There was a connecting door between rooms 15 and 16 wasn't there?"

131

"Yes ... we lived as much in one as the other ... since we cooked together to save money ..."

"Did you know Lieb before he joined the Powell Circus?"

"No! He came directly from England, he said, and we had never performed there."

"Did he ever talk about marrying Henny?"

"Him? ... Ah! No! ... He was a womanizer ... he would chase any skirt ..."

"He was the highest paid member of the circus, was he not?"

"Apparently. Which proves that it's not talent that ..."

"You were supposed to leave the Gambetta Hotel early in the morning on the 19th. Were your bags ready?"

"Yes. We had packed our trunks on the 18th in the afternoon ..."

"And they were supposed to be picked up early in the morning, weren't they? ..."

During this questioning, Timmermans strained so hard to think that he was blue in the face.

"When you saw your niece for the last time, before she left for Paris with Lieb, what coat was she wearing? ... Her winter coat? ..."

"No! It was rather mild ... For two weeks, she had worn a green suit that she had just had made for her ... as she was quite *coquette* ... she would spend as much on her clothes as we spent on ..."

"How would you describe her winter coat?"

"Brown, with fur ... She had burned the bottom of it when she stepped too close to a pot, but this was not so noticeable ..."

"Could you bring it to me?"

"How could I bring it to you if Henny took all her things ..."

"Of course! ... Did your windows look out on the Place de Paris?"

"You really can't provide me with an article of clothing or

underwear that your niece could have worn? Or even some shoes ... how many pairs did she own?"

"Three ... But all we have left are her circus clothes ... They are with ours, in the Powell wagons ..."

"Do you know which movie theater Henny went to?"

"How would we know that?"

"Of course, you never went into Henny's room. You wouldn't be able to tell me where she put her trunk?"

"No ..."

"Your trunk was at the foot of the bed? ..."

"One of the two. The other one was in a corner."

"Did the wicker one contain any underwear?"

"Yes! It was already tied up ..."

"Did Mademoiselle Henny know how to swim?"

"A little ..."

"Do you still have family?"

"My husband's cousin ...But we no longer see him ...We write post-cards to each other from time to time."

"A performer?"

"A farmer, in Warns, not far from Workum ..."

"You didn't need any money when the crime was committed, did you?"

"What for? We had just gotten our weekly paycheck. And we hardly spent anything ..."

"On the 19th, you only had seventy-five francs on you ..."

"Which proves that we're innocent! You don't kill for nothing ..."

Madame Timmermans was animated. She looked at her husband with a certain pride. She seemed to be saying: "You see! ... All you need to do is know how to answer the questions ..."

Monsieur Froget's last question deflated her. "How much time did you spend at the window?"

And he closed his dossier.

⁜ ⁜ ⁜

As though he were a pupil reciting a lesson for a school teacher, Monsieur Froget without so much as even looking at the accused:

"As circus and music-hall artists, you fall first in what the profession calls, I believe, jacks-of-all-trade. And you also traded in swindling and thievery. Without your niece, you wouldn't even have been able to perform your act.

"On the 18th, she goes off with Lieb, who has just picked up a significant pay check. You, on the other hand, had just received a rather modest sum. You are convinced he won't be returning before midnight. You go into his room. You take about three hundred francs.

"Henny returns with her lover. Lieb, noticing the theft, is suspicious of you, bursts into your bedroom and is no doubt about to execute justice with his fists. Seized with panic, you, Timmermans, lunge for his throat. Perhaps you had no intention of killing him? He dies nonetheless and there you are, all three of you, trembling before the body. Taking the body back downstairs, without noise, locking it up in the trunk, *with the stolen money, so that no one would suspect a robbery attempt, and therefore suspect you,* and taking him all the way to the Marne river — all that was child's play. Henny would disappear at the same time, would go hide out somewhere in Holland, so successfully that people would think that she had been kidnaped. You, Madame Timmerman, were posted by the window, in order to open the front door for your husband when he came home."

It was quite a scene. The man started to bitterly spout invectives at his wife in Dutch. She barked in both languages. And all the while, Monsieur Froget wrote in his notebook:

"*Proof:* The Timmermans claim not to have seen Henny who, nevertheless, had taken *all of her belongings*, including a big winter coat and several pairs of shoes. Yet, in actual fact, she possesses but one piece of hand luggage. And the *family* suitcases had been packed the night before, the trunks had been locked and tied. In other words, she must have fatally awakened her uncle and aunt in order to take what was hers from the trunk.

"They deny this! They therefore have an important reason to appear not to be aware of the fact that she left *on her own volition.*

"*Assumptions:* The murderer could not have acted alone, as someone, upon entering, had to have opened the inside door for him. The Timmermans's room has a view of the Place de Paris.

"Timmermans who, on his bicycle, carries both women on his shoulders, is capable of carrying the trunks, which weigh over a hundred kilos, on his shoulders.

"Lieb had been robbed before the murder, as is proved by the scattered notes in the trunk. They had been placed there only after the crime had been committed to avert any notion of theft. And the Timmermans were used to committing petty larceny.

"The Timmermans, who had just picked up their paycheck, have only seventy-five francs on them the day after the crime, since they had to give Henny some money for her trip."

In the margins, written in red ink: "The crime of a terrified coward."

Timmermans tried to pass himself off as a madman and in so doing benefitted from reasonable doubt which at least saved his neck from the guillotine.

The Eleventh Culprit

THE PACHA

THE PACHA

"I WILL grant you, dear sir, that you are an intelligent man, and even a rising magistrate ..."

These words alone, spoken to Monsieur Froget whose icy face, crowned by his white hair, could be mistaken for the face of old age itself in all its immutability and austerity, were incredibly ludicrous in and of themselves.

The accused, however, continued with curt gestures from his hands which were heavy with jewels. "... But you would honor me by admitting that, from your point of view, I am as intelligent as you are. For forty years now I've been haunting the capital cities of the world. Why would you now have expect me to fall into the trap of a few more or less cunning questions, even if I were guilty?"

He straightened a black diamond mounted in a signet ring and added with similar flippancy: "But you must believe that I have not committed murder! Allow me, by the way, to remind you of statistics from your *Police Judiciare* that my lawyer provided me with. They indicate that out of a hundred denunciations brought forth by 'working girls,' there are about ninety nine that are false from top to bottom."

Not a trace of emotion, worry or fear. A perfect tranquility which was not faked. In fact, as an accused but free man, he arrived at the Grand Hotel at that very moment in a hired chauffeur-driven car, and before entering the judge's chambers, he had conferred with his attorney who was one of the three most celebrated lawyers on the Parisian bar.

THE 13 CULPRITS

The women who had given their depositions called him "the Pacha." His real name was Enesco, which was followed by a litany of difficult names. He was born in Stamboul, but his nationality was hard to pin down, as he had lived throughout the entire world and still spent three months of the year in Paris; he was seen just as frequently in Cairo, in Constantinople, the Indies and even in the Far East.

He was very rich. He owed his wealth to his father who had been one of the biggest merchants in Asia Minor before the war. He was big, strong, a little on the fat side, with skin that was so white that women envied him, and that his brilliant black hair highlighted. His entire being — complexion and clothes, nails and eyebrows, teeth and jewels — was cared for to such a degree that Westerners either ignored or condemned it. He put on a lot of cologne to boot! And everything that belonged to him — his cigarette holder, his clothing, his little notebook that he took out of his pocket from time to time, the slightest object, the flimsiest trinket — all were wonderful.

In order to establish the grounds for the indictment, Monsieur Froget had to interrogate prostitutes: nine to be exact, semi-high class, headquartered in one of the great cafés on the boulevard des Capucines. One of them had spoken so loudly in front of a vice-squad detective that she had set off the machinery of justice.

In sum, the nine women had each, one or more times, been taken home by the Pacha to his apartment in the Grand Hotel. They all complained about having been subjected to more or less cruel treatment.

There was a long list, recorded in Monsieur Froget's calm and precise handwriting. The nine women had one accusation in common: the Pacha enjoyed lightly burning their skin with a lit cigar in order to make them tremble. Some had gotten angry. He was quick to pay them enough money so that they would agree to be quiet. Others had been more resigned. But, faced with his increasingly extravagant demands, they gave up one by one.

"A cat! ..." they said of him. "He's made of honey. He smiles. And suddenly there are strange sparks coming from his eyes. He doesn't stop smiling, but at the same time, he becomes horrible, and you really feel as though he could be capable of anything if you were to make him angry ..."

The facts: on June 6th, Maria Lebesque, better known as Mia on the *Grands Boulevards*, twenty-two years old, blonde, thin, pretty, previously married to a dentist from Lyon and only recently engaged in prostitution, discusses the Pacha with her colleagues as she sees him sitting down at a café.

It's the first time she sees the man from Stamboul. The others speak to him with their voices lowered. She laughs. "You're all a bunch of idiots, you know! As for me, a guy like that, I lead him by the nose and do with him as I please."

"You'll see, you'll be terrified sooner or later ..."

Maria Lebesque gets up, with her silk coat sticking to her thighs, brushes against the Pacha, sits down at the table next to his. Fifteen minutes later, she enters the Grand Hotel with him. Nobody sees her at night. Nor the next day. A friend of hers inquires about her whereabouts on the rue Caulaincourt where Mia owns a small apartment. She never returned.

The doorman at the Grand Hotel is rather imprecise: "At five o'clock in the afternoon, the hall is so busy at teatime that I didn't notice anything. But, at around seven o'clock, Monsieur Enesco went out alone. He came back less than a half an hour later with a gentleman who stayed up there for an hour."

"Did he go back out with the visitor?"

"No ..."

"And at that moment? ..."

"I didn't see him myself, but a messenger had seen him get into a taxi with a woman on his arm."

The messenger answers the question categorically.

"Was the woman alive?"

"*Parbleu*! She was *walking* ..."

❖ ❖ ❖

The date on the calendar is now the 26th of June. For three weeks, she is looked for everywhere. No body is found that corresponds to Maria Lebesque's description. The man who had visited Enesco is not found either.

"A friend whose name I don't even know!" says the latter. "I met him in a bar. I saw him from time to time, holding a cocktail. I invited him over to smoke a Havana cigar."

"Was Mia still there ..."

"Yes ... she was exhausted ... She had asked my permission to lie down for an hour or two on my couch...Perhaps she had had too much to drink ..."

"Did one of the boys working in the hotel serve you drinks?"

"No! I always have some liqueurs in my room ..." He answers condescendingly. A light smile floats across his lips while he plays with his rings, removes some dirt that from beneath a fingernail.

"How is it that you took a cab when you went out with Maria Lebesque when you had a chauffeur-driven car at your disposal?"

"This happens quite frequently. I would have had to phone the garage ..."

"You claim to have dropped her off at the Place Clichy, in other words two hundred meters from where she lives. Why didn't you take her all the way to her door?"

A smile showing slight pity ..."You forget that I owed her nothing ... Keep in mind that we're talking about a ..." A small hand gesture completes his thought.

"The cab driver was never found ..."

"Which proves that he wasn't driving a corpse around. Otherwise, he would have remembered ..."

"I suppose you do not deny what nine witnesses reproach you for?"

The smile becomes sharper. There is really something feline about it, and simultaneously extremely intelligent, in its physiognomy. A sonorous voice murmurs: "Come now, my dear sir ..." Doesn't he rather mean: "How can you be bothered with these fantasies?"

Promptly, he starts speaking again: "It doesn't take much to provoke an accusation, does it? No corpse! What could I have done with the body? And this didn't take place in an isolated villa, a townhouse, not even an ordinary apartment but in one of the busiest sections of Paris ..."

"You could have killed her *after...*"

"Why? ... Can I offer you a cigar?"

"Thank you ..."

He lights one, with a series of precious gestures. He has his monogram on his ring. His head tilted backwards, he watches as the smoke rises.

Monsieur Froget's hands are as white as his interlocutor's, but there is a coldness to their whiteness, scratched with bruises, and tipped with square fingernails which shuffle some papers. The prosecutor had warned him. It was the last interrogation. If he doesn't come up with some clear results, the case will be filed away.

"In what bar did you meet the friend you brought back with you to the hotel?"

"Near the Madeleine ... *Le Cristal*, I believe ..."

"You weren't seen in any of the bars in that neighborhood that night. Just a moment ... Was this an elegant friend?"

"But of course ... I don't see how ..."

"French?"

"I think so ..."

"Are you a morphine addict?"

"Not in the least. I have a rather nice collection of vices, as you are well aware, but that one isn't included ..."

"How do you explain the syringe that was found at your place in a cracked glass, without a needle, and measuring five cubic centimeters?"

"They found that at my place?"

"In the wastepaper basket ..."

"I didn't know that ... Unless Mia ... Indeed, I noticed several blue marks on her thighs. All you would have to do is question her, when you find her ..."

"The syringe didn't work. It had no doubt exploded at the time it was being dipped in boiling water."

"That's the first I have heard of it."

"The investigation has established that you were formally introduced to the best of circles."

Enesco bowed mockingly.

"We couldn't find a single oddball among your acquaintances."

Same bow. Monsieur Froget began to feel the stale fragrance emanating from the accused's hair and clothes and which was becoming even more nauseating since it was mixed with the cigar smell. He tapped his desk with the ivory paper cutter and mumbled to himself: "On June 6th and the days that followed, you did not write a single check to anyone we were able to trace. You used to go to the bank each week to withdraw the pocket money you needed. Stop me if I say something that is not correct. Yet, the week of Maria Lebesque's disappearance, you withdrew the usual amount of money."

"I suppose what you're saying is that on that week, I did not have any unusual expenses ..."

"That you did not have any extraordinary expenses, yes! Around four to five hundred francs a day for daily needs ..."

"You're seeing things my way. And I thank you! Because, let's say I did commit murder and then make Mia disappear, with the full complicity of my guest, I would have had to pay him, and then the taxi driver. And those are services that can become quite expensive."

"It has also been established that not a single one of your jewels is missing."

"Thank you once again! ... You continue to defend me ..." And, with great flippancy, half-lord of the manor and half-adventurer: "Come now, leave that alone, dear sir! If you would decide to believe me, we could have ourselves an excellent dinner, you and I and ..."

"Regrettably ... Here is the warrant for your arrest ..."

Enesco thought it was some sort of ruse. He started to snicker. Then his face hardened. His teeth shone. "You think so?" His voice had lost its warm nonchalance. "I suppose you're charging me with murder of a prostitute?"

"No!"

"So ... what crime are you charging me with? ... For what crime?"

"You know the one ..."

"You have to release me."

"I am afraid so"

"All I have to do is I call my lawyer, who'll take care of everything!"

The Pacha could change moods from one second to the next. He was once again made of honey, with a touch of something serious, however, something admiring in his gaze. "My dinner invitation still stands. But you'll have to tell me how you arrived at the truth ..."

"I'll tell you ... without the dinner! ... Just be so kind as to open the window ... the smoke bothers me ..."

Enesco obeyed.

✤ ✤ ✤

"You did not kill Maria Lebesque and I will first demonstrate this by absurdity, as we say in geometry:

"1. Having committed a murder, especially under such odious circumstances, you would have had the time to leave France from the 6th to the 21st of June as nothing important was holding you back.

"2. You would have allowed a man in your hotel room only if he had been an accomplice.

"3. You did not frequent the sleazy parts of Paris and it is more or less impossible, under these circumstances, in a half an hour, to find an individual who would be able to help you in such a matter, especially an elegant individual who could pass for a gentleman, especially in the Grand Hotel where they know how to recognize them.

"4. Such a man would have to be paid a large fee, and cash down. Yet, you signed no check, nor did you deposit any money, nor give away any jewel.

"5. Two people would have been required to remove a corpse from the hotel by passing it off as a living person, each one holding up one of the arms of the deceased. Therefore, Maria Lebesque was alive when she left the Grand Hotel. She followed you on her own volition.

"Would you tell me what kind of elegant man one could find at a moment's notice in the middle of Paris, who might be able to offer a certain assistance and who would then remain silent about it afterwards? *A doctor!* He is bound by professional confidentially. The glass syringe — without a needle, which means that the needle had been taken away with the rest of the kit! — proves that he had been in your room. Note that individuals usually use nickel-plated syringes and that, for morphine, for example, only one cubic centimeter instruments are used. He treated Maria Lebesque, whom you had wounded, but he didn't help move her for you. You had to do that on your own."

Monsieur Froget fired a glance at his papers.

"Allow me to summarize: Mia follows you with the idea of pushing you over the edge and then taking advantage of that occasion. Given your previous history with prostitutes, it is quite likely that you would have let yourself be carried away by your impulses. You wounded her with the burning cigar. What now becomes important is for you to avoid any legal ramifications. *You did not know that her friends know that she is at your place and that they'll talk.* You go to find a doctor. You promise a huge amount of money to your victim. You take her either to a clinic, or elsewhere, where she will have to remain until she is completely healed. I have reason to believe that it was a clinic in this case, the one the doctor who came to the hotel worked in, because you didn't pay him. You therefore had to see him again. If you didn't tell the truth when we started to get to you it was because you knew we wouldn't be able to find any evidence against you; although if you admitted that you inflicted the wounds, you would end up in the court of summary jurisdiction where the judges have the upper hand. It is true that Maria Lebesque would refuse to press charges against you, that you would pull strings ..."

And Monsieur Froget made a note for himself in his notebook:

"*Proof:* the syringe that Enesco maintains he knew nothing about and that he tries to attribute to Maria, even though it was a model that she could not have had access to herself. A doctor arrived. Therefore there is a wound or a disease that he isn't talking about, and that he will consequently have to hide.

"*Assumptions:* Absence of any payments. The fact that the cab driver had not come to the police, *because he performed a normal errand and drove the patient to a known clinic.* Enesco's presence in Paris after June 6th. The unlikelihood of his having admitted an unknown visitor to his room when he already had a woman waiting there."

The case was filed away. Maria Lebesque, who received compensation in the amount of a hundred thousand francs, started her own dressmaking shop in Montmartre. She has to take certain precautions, so that no one will know how she received a certain scar.

The Twelfth Culprit

OTTO MÜLLER

OTTO MÜLLER

THE REPORT to the *Polizei Praesidium* of Emden, which Monsieur Froget read to the accused, contained the following:
"Otto Müller, born in Wilhelmshaven in 1889, from a civil-servant family. At sixteen, is hired as a dental assistant in Emden. After his military service, marries Lady Falken, who is ten years older then he is. Moves into a comfortable apartment in Emden and takes out several patents on a type of dental cement which he invented and which he manufactures with his wife and a servant.

"When war is declared, he has four or five patents, including one for an automatic syringe. At the Front in 1915, gets himself attached to a hospital in Cologne. In 1919, is arrested in Hamburg for illegally wearing a major's uniform. Gets divorced and marries a former *café-concert* singer, Elena Schramm. Returns to Emden, tries to jumpstart his business. Borrows some money. Goes bankrupt in 1928. Lives in a hotel with his wife. Seems as though he has no means of making a living. On November 7, 1929, requests a passport to go to Paris. Sets off alone."

Another report that was equally typical from the Research Division in Paris:

"On November 9th, 1929, Otto Müller checks into the Delta Hotel, Place du Delta, and claims to be an engineer. He is still wearing a worn-out Hussars pelisse. Pays for the first week. For the second one, he makes the hotel keeper wait three days. Announces that he will be concluding a major deal in a matter of days. Asks the bellboy about cocaine traffic in Paris. On November 16, tries to sell ten grams

151

in a café in Montmartre. Mistaking him for an informer, the bartender refuses his offer. Muller makes a fresh attempt three days later, offers to sell his drugs at a laughable price. Still does not manage to unload them.

"Visits two or three German expatriates in France, including a dentist, tells them of his new patent, and tries to extract a significant amount of money from them. In vain. Goes back to one of them and after five visits, borrows two hundred francs.

"Tries to get a job as an interpreter at a fancy hotel. Pays for his room with increasing irregularity. The hotel keeper is of the opinion that he is probably not eating every day.

"Two or three times a week, he is seen on the rue d'Hauteville at the residence of Helmut Karr, a former colleague from Wilhelmshaven, who owns a small business selling tacky trinkets: pencil-holders, cheap pens, ebonite nick-knacks, fool's gold, imitation ivory and amber, etc. ...

"Helmut Karr, who had been naturalized since 1911, is fifty-five years old. He is a widower. The premises consist of a boutique and, directly in back, a tiny dwelling. Karr eats in a neighborhood restaurant. He has an employee who leaves work at six o'clock. In the evenings, with his shutters closed, Karr usually stayed in the boutique where he would do his bookkeeping. After a look at his records, it would seem that, despite his shabby-looking appearances and modest shopkeeper's lifestyle, he was extremely prosperous.

"On several occasions, the employee, who is French, had heard Otto Müller insist on having Karr lend him money. One day, he even offered to work for him as a warehouseman, or to travel for his trinkets."

As an aside: "The sand pebbles that were found in Müller's pelisse could have come only from the Quai de Tournelles from a houseboat that had been unloading there since November 26."

⁘ ⁘ ⁘

Müller was a big fellow with a shaven head, bushy, dark eyebrows and a hardened gaze. He was not fat, but to look at his clothes which floated all over him, one could deduce that he had recently lost a lot of weight. He had gray unshaven cheeks. He wore his worn pelisse, a celluloid detachable collar and a clip-on tie.

"To put it bluntly," Monsieur Froget observed as he pushed his papers aside, "you've spent your entire life trying to find ways to make your jackpot."

"I was rich, at times ..."

"When your first wife brought you some money, you were! Would you like to tell me what you were doing on November 27th at six o'clock in the evening?"

"I went to the movies. Then, I went to bed, at the Delta Hotel."

"At three o'clock in the morning ..."

"*Pardon*, a little after midnight ..."

"The floor waiter claims that he opened the door for only one person who had not cried out his name, and that was at three o'clock in the morning."

"How would he have known? He's half-asleep when he opens the door."

Monsieur Forget seizes and carefully examines the pictures that were taken by the Criminal Records Office on the Rue d'Hauteville. They showed Karr's boutique after it had been ransacked, drawers opened, papers strewn about the counter and on the floor. On the floor, behind the counter, a corpse was bent in half, the gray hair was stuck to the scalp: it was Karr's body, just as the employee had found him the next morning at eight o'clock. The merchant was in his slippers. The forensic pathologist had attributed the death to a heavy blow to the head from a club, which had been administered with a rare sense of precision, as though the murderer had had all the time in the world. Nonetheless, the death had not been instantaneous: Karr had remained alive for nearly three hours, paralyzed and unable to cry for help.

The murder had been committed around nine thirty in the evening. *Yet, even though Karr was dead, there was then a second blow to the temples, at around midnight.*

Otto Müller had been arrested the next day, after accusations brought against him by the employee who, on the 26th, had witnessed a scene between Müller and Karr, which, again, was over money.

Neither the club, nor any other piece of evidence worthy of a conviction were found.

Karr was used to keeping around three to five thousand francs at home, without counting the notes. In his wallet, three thousand two hundred francs were found, as well as a document signed by Müller, attesting to his having received a five hundred franc loan on the 25th.

The employee gave troubling answers to the questions he was asked.

"Did Karr usually keep money in his wallet?"

"Never! The money was always kept in a metal box that was placed behind the counter, by day, and in the employer's room at night."

"Did he have to go to the bank the day after?"

"He didn't say anything about that. It wasn't a pay day."

"Was the three thousand two hundred franc figure the same

amount that was in the boutique that night?"

"I don't know. I worked in the warehouse mostly."

Otto Müller was neither humble nor arrogant. He was making a visible effort to fully understand the significance of the questions he was asked, and was looking for the right words to answer them. He did not speak impeccable French. When he used certain terms that he was not sure about, he would pause, look at the judge as though he were seeking some sort of approval.

"On the 25th, you received five hundred francs from Karr. We found the receipt in his pocket. The employee claims that his boss never handed you such large amounts of money. A few days earlier, Karr literally threw a pack of twenty francs in your face as he told you to go to Hell a thousand times over. Why was he suddenly so generous on the 25th?"

"Because I promised him that I would go back to Emden."

"With the money he gave you?"

"Yes."

"Even though you still owed three hundred and twenty francs to the hotel! There would not be enough left for your trip ..."

"I intended to leave without paying for the room."

"Why didn't you go?"

"I was afraid the boss would press charges against me and I would be stopped at the border."

"On the day of your arrest, on the 28th to be exact, how much was left from the bundle of cash?"

"A hundred and forty francs."

"After which, to put it bluntly, you were at the end of your rope?"

"I could still work."

"Why didn't you do it earlier?"

Otto Müller remains silent, sighs, as though he were resigned to worst possible criticism.

"Why would I have killed Karr?" he asks finally.

"Did you know that he used to keep his money in a metal box?"

"Yes! He took out the five hundred francs from that box."

"The box had a combination lock, like a safe. Did you know the password?"

"No ..."

"The box wasn't found on the rue d'Hauteville!"

"I don't know."

"Witnesses, including the owner of the corner café, have testified that they saw a light at Karr's place until around one in the morning. They could see it through a crack in the shutters. But by morning, the electricity was off."

"I don't know."

"The last train for Belgium and Germany departs at half past eleven out of the Gare du Nord station."

"I don't know."

"*Pardon!*" On the morning of the 26th, you purchased a train schedule."

"Because I promised Karr that I would leave."

"So you knew what time the train left ... It's the only one in Cologne to have a connection for Bremen and Emden ..."

"I had forgotten that."

"No fingerprints were found on the premises. But there is proof that the murderer did not use rubber gloves. He had carefully wiped off every object he touched. This precaution must have taken him more than an hour."

"I had no motive to kill Karr. I'm innocent."

"Sea sand was found on your pelisse. As of November 13, this kind of sand was being unloaded off the Quai des Tournelles. When did you go to the Quai des Tournelles?"

"A week before my arrest, it was on a Monday, I believe. Around the 17th. I had wanted to commit suicide. I sat on a rock for a longtime watching the barges go by."

"You didn't go to the Quai des Tournelles on the night of the murder?"

"No. I was at the movies."

"And the day after?"

"No! In fact, two detectives came by to pick me up a little before midnight."

"You had just flushed your ten grams of cocaine down the toilet."

"Because I was unable to sell them ..."

"You usually had a five-blade Swiss knife on you. What did you do with it?"

"I don't know. I must have lost it. Unless of course it was stolen by one of the bellboys at the hotel."

"What would you do if I let you walk out of here a free man?"

"I would take the next train to Emden. I've had it with Paris."

"Who sewed your tie back together?"

"I don't understand."

Monsieur Froget pointed to a small black thread which was sticking out.

"I did ..."

"You know how to sew? And you had needles, a thimble, a thread in your room?"

"Like any traveler."

157

"Hand it over ..."

Müller's complexion became jaundiced all of a sudden. His eyes blurred. He threw his tie onto the table and put his head in his two hands.

A thousand franc note had been sewn between the two layers of cloth. Monsieur Froget sensed that there was no point in speaking to the man who had just crumbled before him; he would not have heard a thing. Peacefully, he jotted down:

"*Proof:* Müller insists that he had gone to the Quai des Tournelles a week before the crime had been committed, *even though there was no sea sand at that location before the 26th.* Therefore, he must have been there on the night of the murder, but makes sure that his presence along the Seine goes unnoticed. Yet, Karr's metal box had not been found.

"*Assumptions:* An hour before his arrest, and while the public is still unaware of the murder, Müller gets rid of the cocaine. *And so he expects to be investigated.*

"Existence of the document attesting to the five hundred franc debt, even though the employee asserts that Müller asked Karr for money the day after that money would have been deposited. It's a way for Müller to cast suspicion away from himself. Firstly, this explains why he has pocket money on him. Then, he hopes that people would think that if he were the murderer he would have destroyed that receipt.

"*Facts:* Müller mulls over his plan, writes the receipt with which he will arm himself, along with a club, and enters the boutique at night. Strikes Karr right away as he is slumped over his desk. He is nervous, worried. He seizes the metal box, looks for the key in vain, and runs away with it. Once he is at the Quai des Tournelles, he breaks it open with the help of his knife. He expected, no doubt, to catch the last train, so that he could be in Germany when the crime would be discovered. But the box resisted for a long time. Müller misses his train. He starts to panic, roams the city, anticipates that the employee would point the figure at him.

"It is at that point that he returns to the rue d'Hauteville. It's midnight, or shortly thereafter. The body is still warm. Müller fears he might recover and strikes him for a second time. Then, to cover his tracks, he decides to put some of the money back. He keeps only a thousand franc note. The smashed box is at the bottom of the Seine. The murderer slides the notes into the dead man's wallet, adds to the disarray, erases the fingerprints, turns off the light and takes off. Cautious to the utmost degree, he sews the bill into his tie once he is back in his room. He can rest easier with the knowledge that he has not left a single clue behind him.

"A crime that is both loathsome and scientific perpetrated by a mediocre, complicated and self-absorbed individual."

The Thirteenth Culprit

BUS

BUS

THE FIRST document to be rushed to all the European police stations was a copy of the memorandum that was written by the New York Police Department and published in newspapers all over America:

"1000 dollar reward to anyone with information leading to the arrest of Ronald Morton, also known as Bus, a black man living in Harlem and working as a waiter in a restaurant. Apparent age: twenty-five. Tall. Skinny legs. Throws out his chest. Low forehead.

"On May 21st, at the Black and White Bar, Bus, in the midst of a heated discussion, fired four shots into the barman, then at the patrons who wanted to intervene. Two dead, one wounded. He then escaped into the neighborhood where he shot the officer in charge of the district, who was trying to block his way, and, late that night, as he was hunted in a furnished apartment, he literally gunned down two police officers before fleeing along the rooftops. There is every reason to believe that he was not able to leave the city."

Second document: copy of a wireless transmission from the American authorities on board the *Mauritania*.

"A Negro was spotted aboard traveling illegally. It seems as though he got on from a lifeboat. The crew chased him. Fired two shots. One death. Extremely agile, seems to know the boat backwards and forwards, he disappeared. Patrols are sent out day and night."

Another message from the American authorities:

"Negro is spotted for a second time in a 2nd Class compartment. Disappeared."

From the *Mauritania* to the French Police:

"Negro wanted in New York for series of murders aboard. Escaped capture.   One sailor dead.   Urge surveillance of disembarkation."

And the chain continued, link by link.

Mobile Squad in Le Havre to the *Police Judiciaire* in Paris, May 30:

"Searched *Mauritania*.   Found nothing.   At six o'clock in the evening, a Negro is spotted in the red-light district.   Will keep you updated."

Also from the Mobile Squad to the *Police Judiciare*.

"Hectic night.   Negro spotted three times.   Shootout on the rue Saint-Jacques.   A woman wounded.   We're watching all train stations and boat departures."

Second telegram, same date, two hours later:

"Bus arrested as he is entering the train station with a first class ticket to Paris.   No employee had handed him the ticket.   No resistance.   Feigns idiocy."

✜ ✜ ✜

June 5th.

A dog would have had to wander the streets of a city for days and nights, hungry, battered blows and trash aimed at the head, he would have had to have been hunted down by the children themselves, and then they would have abandoned him with such contempt for him to look as pitiful, as desperately humble as Bus, the Negro — the Negro that Monsieur Froget had before him in his Palais de Justice chambers.

The guards who had brought him over told him to sit down but he didn't understand them, or perhaps pretended not to understand them. They had pushed him around a little and he had slipped to the edge of the chair in a twisted position.   He remained precariously seated, his pupils were dilated, his eyelids swollen, his complexion gray and sweaty. One thing was sure: he had been worked over. But nothing was found to indicate that he was a thief. He hadn't uttered a single word for four days since his arrest. He just stared straight ahead stubbornly, or stupidly, with both despair and resignation.

"When you decide to stop this nonsense ..." the policemen shouted.

And then, wham! ...

He was in pretty bad shape, that was a fact. His clothes were dirty and torn. Swollen face. Scratches to his hands and wrists.

Once he was before Monsieur Froget, he seemed to burst into tears. And incidentally the tears on his cheeks were real but silent. One of them was quivering on the dried blood from one of his scratches. From time to time, he would sniffle, as softly as possible, as though he were afraid he might be punished by new blows.

A supplementary cablegram from New York read:

"Originally from the Belgian Congo. Worked in Southern plantations for several years. Starts drinking in Harlem, becomes violent, but commits no crime before May 21 nor any serious misdemeanor at all. He was drunk during the series of murders. The bullets were fired from a Colt 12-mm revolver, a 1913 model, with cylinder. The experts had determined that one of the grooves of the rifling must be irregular. Wearing a light gray three piece suit. Pants with leather belt without suspenders. Greenish socks. Polished black shoes. Had around three hundred dollars on him on the night of the crime."

A Colt 12-mm revolver, a 1913 model, with an empty barrel had been found in the pockets of the Negro who sat collapsed in front of Monsieur Froget. Bus was out of bullets. The Parisian expert, who had examined the weapon, certified that one of the grooves in the rifling had been falsified.

And Bus remained silent, waited for some blows, no doubt. One could see his belly panting like a bird that one holds in one's hand.

The American police continued: "Speaks fluent English and understands Spanish and Italian."

He had been interrogated in each of these three languages, with no results. His features had been scrutinized. Not a single tremor! There was something inhuman, pitiful, and revolting all at once! Monsieur Froget, who could speak only French, would not allow himself the absurdity of trying to speak another language. All he wanted was his man before him.

Uncharacteristically, he did not remain seated, with one shoulder a little higher than the other, in his favorite position. He walked up and down, as though under the spell of a fever. He rubbed his white and terribly dry hands, one against the other, mechanically, to the point where they sounded like crumpled paper. And from time to time, he approached his desk, read through a document, a note.

As time passed, the black man imperceptibly lifted his head in wonder, and looked at the old man, who wasn't doing anything to him, with a kind of hope.

Monsieur Froget managed to pluck the following from a report given by the mobile squad in Le Havre: "We were able to seize the following from the Negro's pocket: a revolver, see attached detailed description; a dollar in gold and some loose change; a pack of *Gauloises* with only one missing cigarette. Bus had nothing else on him."

And, further down: "The woman, Elise Claudet, a madam of an establishment called *La Vénus Maritime*, testifies that a Negro wearing a gray three-piece suit spent a part of the night at her place from the 31st of May to the 1st of June. As he was poorly dressed, she urged him to pay up front and he placed a hundred dollar bill on the table. Drinking in the company of two girls in one of the sitting rooms of the house, he produced a revolver with only two bullets left which he made a point of mentioning for the sake of anyone who might attempt to prevent him from having a good time. He spoke in English, a language these women were used to. He insisted that one window remain opened and he made sure he knew what was on the other side of it. Left the house at three o'clock in the morning."

The fifteen page report continued : "The deposition from Julien Groslier, a fifty-five year old salesman living in Le Havre. (It's worth mentioning that Groslier is drunk every night and that he rarely works.)

" 'I was on my way home ...'

" 'At what time?'

" 'Around daybreak ...I was on my way home and I was walking by, not far from the train station, when someone went *Pssst* ... It was a Negro, who was speaking to me in English and who promised me twenty francs if I wanted to pick up a ticket to Paris for him at the ticket booth. I asked for a 1st class one and I found him waiting for me outside.'

" 'How was he dressed?'

" 'I hadn't noticed ...But he was *funny* ...'

" 'What do you mean by that?'

" 'He whistled and when he gave me the twenty francs he was so happy that he stretched it out to fifty. I think that he was *a little dru* ...'

" 'And you?'

" 'Hardly! I drink just enough so that I can forget my troubles ...' "

The employee from the train station specifies that it was six o'clock in the morning when he handed over the ticket. The Negro had been arrested at the tracks of the train station at eight-nineteen.

Deposition from the night watchman from the Blackwell Docks, in Le Havre: "At around three o'clock in the morning, I threw out a damn Negro whom I kicked as he slept in the middle of balls of wool that had been unloaded the night before. He didn't complain."

"How was he dressed?"

"It was dark. And he got the h … out in a split second."

Monsieur Froget went over, looked the accused right in the eyes and Bus jumped up, letting some more tears trickle down his cheeks.

The psychiatric doctors who had subjected him to a preliminary examination claimed that they could diagnose him only after he had been placed under observation. In any case, Bus hadn't been stricken with a serious illness. There were no signs of insanity.

The magistrate suddenly opened the door and called for a guard. "Take off his shoes."

The Negro offered no resistance. He revealed bloody, swollen feet.

"Has this man been sleeping with his shoes on for several days?"

"Yes, and with all his clothes on …"

His legs, caked with sweat and mud, were thin. There were a few strands of raw wool that had been stuck to them.

Bus was as pitiful and grotesque as ever, sitting on his chair, with his bare feet, and his dangling arms which seemed excessively long. The guard left the room in disgust, holding his own hands away from his body because he had touched the accused's feet.

Having reached a peak of irritation, Monsieur Froget scrambled all of the file's documents which sported a myriad of different letterheads, walked towards the window, retraced his steps. He was about to continue to speak to Bus in the same manner as he had been doing, but he shut his mouth before uttering a single syllable.

And he brusquely opened the door again and called for the guard. "This is a measuring stick ... Do you know how to measure a foot size?"

A few moments later, the guard announced: "It's a forty-six ..."

"The foot? ..."

"Forty four! ... But it's a very fine leather and it's expandable ..."

The Negro stared fixedly at an abrasion on his hand.

"No bits of wool in the cracks in the leather?"

"None ... but some charcoal ... Look! This shoe right here is full ..."

Monsieur Froget shot a look at his desk and his eyes fell on a sentence within the report: "Colt revolver, 12-mm caliber, 1913 model."

"You can leave now!" he said to the guard.

✣ ✣ ✣

It was by chance that I ran into Monsieur Froget that day, less than an hour after what can with difficulty be called the Negro's interrogation. And before finding out what was happening, I noticed that there was something unusual about him, a sort of joy that he did not want to let out, as well as, admittedly, a touch of bitterness.

"I know of nothing more sinister," he told me, "than seeing a person suffer who doesn't know why he is suffering, such as an animal or a simple ..."

It was then that he revealed the case to me, as I have tried to tell it, and concluded: "Right from the start, I had gathered several presumptions of innocence from the man. First of all, the stupid manner in which he allowed himself to be apprehended, *he who had hitherto shown himself to be a master of escape*; then the fact that there were bullets in neither his revolver nor his pockets and that he had nonetheless kept such a compromising weapon; the further fact that this man, who had accumulated quite a list of victims, would allow himself to be chased without protest by a night watchman; the fact that he must have seen that the station was being watched, when he sent someone off to buy his ticket. And I'm omitting some points! As for the proof, I only got it at the end, by accident, by looking at his feet that he couldn't figure out how to make touch the floor.

"He indeed wore polished shoes that were indicated by the American police, but they were two sizes too small! And yet one cannot perform such acrobatics under those conditions. *And above all, Bus, who had money, had no reason to wear shoes that were too short and too narrow for him.*

"Therefore, it wasn't Bus whom I had before me!"

He added after a moment of silence: "Now everything has become simple! No one would dream of innocently playing the role that the accused had played, even for such a sum. And so he had to have been acting naturally. And so he knows neither French, nor English, nor Spanish, nor Italian. He doesn't know anything! Furthermore, he has something on his conscience, since he is not even indignant about the police brutality that was inflicted on him.

"The telephone investigation that I've just performed confirmed my suppositions. We are dealing with an unfortunate Negro from the Upper Congo who had heard so much about Europe that he had but one dream: to come over and make his fortune here. A rather unscrupulous compatriot, working in the storeroom on a cargo ship, made him pay a pretty penny in exchange for his fraudulent passage within the coal supply, and abandoned him in Le Havre without a sou, without the means to communicate with anyone at all.

"The man, who had fallen from the pedestal of his dream, wanders about like an errant soul in pain, sleeps on the docks, feels miserable and guilty, gives up. That night, he is chased out of the stack of wool on which he was sleeping. He must not yet have been wearing Bus's shoes because, while bits of wool had been found on his legs, there were none in the cracks in the leather of worn-out shoes.

"The American meets him, sizes up the truth in the blink of an eye, as he too has African roots, and he had succumbed to the same naive feelings. The real Bus is being hunted down. He's at the end of his rope. What an opportunity! He bamboozles the other black man who suspects nothing and is dazzled by a gold coin and some cigarettes. He gives him clothes, the revolver (prudently unloaded), and sends him off on the next train to Paris, after having procured the ticket for him … Before anyone catches wind of the truth, Bus would have enough time to make it to safety."

I found out later that Monsieur Froget had saved the poor soul from the sentence he would have received for having traveled illegally and that he had personally paid for his return trip to Congo.

As for Bus, he had been killed by three stab wounds a few days later in a brothel in Rouen where he was spending his last dollars.

SOURCES

Through the courtesy of Roland Lacourbe, we include the following information. The 13 short stories were first published in *Détective* magazine in 1930 under the pseudonym Georges Sim. Each story appeared in two parts, the mystery in one issue and the solution in a later one.

"Ziliouk," 13 and 27 March
"M. Rodrigues," 20 March and 3 April
"Mme. Smitt," 27 March and 10 April
"Les 'Flamands'," 3 and 17 April
"Nouchi," 10 and 24 April
"Arnold Schuttringer," 17 April and 1 May
"Waldemar Strvzeski," 24 April and 8 May
"Philippe," 1 and 15 May
"Nicolas," 8 and 22 May
"Les Timmermans," 15 and 29 May
"Le Pacha," 22 May and 5 June
"Otto Müller," 29 May and 12 June
"Bus," 5 and 19 June

The stories appeared in book form as *Les 13 Coupables* by Georges Simenon (Paris: Arthème Fayard & Cie, Èditeurs, 1932).

THE 13 CULPRITS

The first edition in English of *The 13 Culprits* (*Les 13 Coupables*) by Georges Simenon was translated by Peter Schulman. The typeface is 12-point Garamond and the paper is 60-pound Glatfelter Supple Opaque. The first edition comprises approximately 2000 copies in trade softcover, notchbound, and 350 copies sewn in cloth. The cloth copies are signed and numbered by the translator, and are accompanied by a pamphlet containing photographs from the original French edition (1932). The book was printed and bound by Thomson-Shore Inc., Dexter, Michigan, and published by Crippen & Landru Inc., Norfolk, Virginia, in August 2002.

CRIPPEN & LANDRU, PUBLISHERS

P. O. Box 9315

Norfolk, VA 23505

E-mail: CrippenL@Pilot.Infi.Net

Web: www.crippenlandru.com

Crippen & Landru publishes first edition short-story collections by important detective and mystery writers. As of August 2002, the following books have been published (see our website for full details):

Speak of the Devil by John Dickson Carr. 1994. Out of print.

The McCone Files by Marcia Muller. 1995. Signed, numbered clothbound, out of print. Trade softcover, sixth printing, $17.00.

The Darings of the Red Rose by Margery Allingham. 1995. Out of print.

Diagnosis: Impossible, The Problems of Dr. Sam Hawthorne by Edward D. Hoch. 1996. Signed, numbered clothbound, out of print. Trade softcover, second printing, $15.00.

Spadework: A Collection of "Nameless Detective" Stories by Bill Pronzini. 1996. Signed, numbered clothbound, out of print. Trade softcover, out of stock.

Who Killed Father Christmas? And Other Unseasonable Demises by Patricia Moyes. 1996. Signed, numbered clothbound, out of print. A few signed unnumbered cloth overrun copies, $30.00. Trade softcover, $16.00.

My Mother, The Detective: The Complete "Mom" Short Stories, by James Yaffe. 1997. Signed, numbered clothbound, out of print. Trade softcover, $15.00.

In Kensington Gardens Once . . . by H.R.F. Keating. 1997. Signed, numbered clothbound, out of print. Trade softcover, $12.00.

Shoveling Smoke: Selected Mystery Stories by Margaret Maron. 1997. Signed, numbered clothbound, out of print. Trade softcover, out of stock.

The Man Who Hated Banks and Other Mysteries by Michael Gilbert. 1997. Signed, numbered clothbound, out of print. Trade softcover, second printing, $16.00.

The Ripper of Storyville and Other Ben Snow Tales by Edward D. Hoch. 1997. Signed, numbered clothbound, out of print. Trade softcover, out of stock.

Do Not Exceed the Stated Dose by Peter Lovesey. 1998. Signed, numbered clothbound, out of print. Trade softcover, $16.00.

Renowned Be Thy Grave; Or, The Murderous Miss Mooney by P.M. Carlson. 1998. Signed, numbered clothbound, out of print. Trade softcover, $16.00.

Carpenter and Quincannon, Professional Detective Services by Bill Pronzini. 1998. Signed, numbered clothbound, out of print. Trade softcover, second printing, $16.00.

Not Safe After Dark and Other Stories by Peter Robinson. 1998. Signed, numbered clothbound, out of print. Trade softcover, second printing, $16.00.

The Concise Cuddy, A Collection of John Francis Cuddy Stories by Jeremiah Healy. 1998. Signed, numbered clothbound, out of print. Trade softcover, out of stock.

One Night Stands by Lawrence Block. 1999. Out of print.

All Creatures Dark and Dangerous by Doug Allyn. 1999. Signed, numbered clothbound, out of print. Trade softcover, $16.00.

Famous Blue Raincoat: Mystery Stories by Ed Gorman. 1999. Signed, numbered clothbound, out of print. A few signed unnumbered cloth overrun copies, $30.00. Trade softcover, $17.00.

The Tragedy of Errors and Others by Ellery Queen. 1999. Numbered clothbound, out of print. Trade softcover, second printing, $16.00.

McCone and Friends by Marcia Muller. 2000. Signed, numbered clothbound, out of print. Trade softcover, third printing, $16.00.

Challenge the Widow Maker and Other Stories of People in Peril by Clark Howard. 2000. Signed, numbered clothbound, out of print. Trade softcover, $16.00.

The Velvet Touch: Nick Velvet Stories by Edward D. Hoch. 2000. Signed, numbered clothbound, out of print. Trade softcover, $16.00.

Fortune's World by Michael Collins. 2000. Signed, numbered clothbound, out of print. Trade softcover, $16.00.

Long Live the Dead: Tales from Black Mask by Hugh B. Cave. 2000. Signed, numbered clothbound, out of print. Trade softcover, second printing, $16.00.

Tales Out of School: Mystery Stories by Carolyn Wheat. 2000. Signed, numbered clothbound, out of print. Trade softcover, $16.00.

Stakeout on Page Street and Other DKA Files by Joe Gores. 2000. Signed, numbered clothbound, out of print. Trade softcover, second printing, $16.00.

Strangers in Town: Three Newly Discovered Mysteries by Ross Macdonald, edited by Tom Nolan. 2001. Numbered clothbound, out of print. Trade softcover, second printing, $15.00.

The Celestial Buffet and Other Morsels of Murder by Susan Dunlap. 2001. Signed, numbered clothbound, out of print. Trade softcover, $16.00.

Kisses of Death: A Nathan Heller Casebook by Max Allan Collins. 2001. Trade softcover, second printing, $17.00.

The Old Spies Club and Other Intrigues of Rand by Edward D. Hoch. 2001. Signed, numbered clothbound, out of print. A few signed unnumbered cloth overrun copies, $32.00. Trade softcover, $17.00.

Adam and Eve on a Raft: Mystery Stories by Ron Goulart. 2001. Signed, numbered clothbound, $42.00. Trade softcover, $17.00.

The Sedgemoor Strangler and Other Stories of Crime by Peter Lovesey. 2001. Signed, numbered clothbound, out of print. Trade softcover, $17.00.

The Reluctant Detective and Other Stories by Michael Z. Lewin. 2001. Signed, numbered clothbound, $42.00. Trade softcover, $17.00.

The Lost Cases of Ed London by Lawrence Block. 2001. Published only in signed, numbered clothbound, $42.00.

Nine Sons: Collected Mysteries by Wendy Hornsby. 2002. Signed, numbered clothbound, out of print. A few signed unnumbered cloth overrun copies, $32.00. Trade softcover, $16.00.

The Newtonian Egg and Other Cases of Rolf le Roux by Peter Godfrey. 2002. [A "Crippen & Landru Lost Classic"]. Clothbound, $25.00. Trade softcover, $15.00.

The Curious Conspiracy and Other Crimes by Michael Gilbert. 2002. Signed, numbered clothbound, $42.00. Trade softcover, $17.00.

Murder, Mystery and Malone by Craig Rice, edited by Jeffrey A. Marks. 2002. [A "Crippen & Landru Lost Classic"]. Clothbound, $27.00. Trade softcover, $17.00.

The Sleuth of Baghdad: The Inspector Chafik Stories by Charles B. Child. 2002. [A "Crippen & Landru Lost Classic"]. Clothbound, $27.00. Trade softcover, $17.00.

The Thirteen Culprits by Georges Simenon, translated by Peter Schulman. 2002. Numbered clothbound, $37.00. Trade softcover, $16.00.

Forthcoming Short-Story Collections

The Dark Snow and Other Stories by Brendan DuBois.

Jo Gar's Casebook by Raoul Whitfield, edited by Keith Alan Deutsch [published with Black Mask Press].

Come Into My Parlor: Stories from Detective Fiction Weekly by Hugh B. Cave.

Hildegarde Withers: Uncollected Riddles by Stuart Palmer [A "Crippen & Landru Lost Classic"].

The Iron Angel and Other Tales of Michael Vlado by Edward D. Hoch.

One of a Kind: Collected Mystery Stories by Eric Wright.

Problems Solved by Bill Pronzini and Barry N. Malzberg.

Cuddy Plus One by Jeremiah Healy.

The Spotted Cat and Other Mysteries from the Casebook of Inspector Cockrill by Christianna Brand, edited by Tony Medawar [A "Crippen & Landru Lost Classic"].

Kill the Umpire: The Calls of Ed Gorgon by Jon L. Breen.

Banner Crimes by Joseph Commings, edited by Robert Adey [A "Crippen & Landru Lost Classic"].

Fourteen Slayers by Paul Cain, edited by Max Allan Collins and Lynn Myers [published with Black Mask Press].

Marksman and Other Stories by William Campbell Gault, edited by Bill Pronzini [A "Crippen & Landru Lost Classic"].

The Adventure of the Murdered Moths and Other Radio Mysteries by Ellery Queen.

Karmesin, The World's Greatest Thief — Or Most Outrageous Liar by Gerald Kersh, edited by Paul Duncan [A "Crippen & Landru Lost Classic"].

The Mankiller of Poojeegai and Other Mysteries by Walter Satterthwait.

You'll Die Laughing by Norbert Davis, edited by Bill Pronzini [published with Black Mask Press].

The Couple Next Door: Collected Mystery Short Stories by Margaret Millar, edited by Tom Nolan [A "Crippen & Landru Lost Classic"].

Hoch's Ladies by Edward D. Hoch.

Murder — All Kinds by William L. DeAndrea [A "Crippen & Landru Lost Classic"].

A Pocketful of Noses: Stories of One Ganelon or Another by James Powell.

Tough As They Come by Frederick Nebel, edited by Rob Preston [published with Black Mask Press].

Slot-Machine Kelly: Early Private-Eye Stories by Michael Collins.

Murder! 'Orrible Murder! by Amy Myers.

More Things Impossible: The Second Casebook of Dr. Sam Hawthorne, by Edward D. Hoch.

The Confessions of Owen Keane by Terence Faherty.

Murders and Other Confusions: The Chronicles of Susana, Lady Appleton, Sixteenth-Century Gentlewoman, Herbalist, and Sleuth by Kathy Lynn Emerson.

Crippen & Landru offers discounts to individuals and institutions who place Standing Order Subscriptions for its forthcoming publications, either the Regular Series or the Lost Classics or (preferably) both. Collectors can thereby guarantee receiving limited editions, and readers won't miss any favorite stories. Standing Order Subscribers receive a specially commissioned story in a deluxe edition as a gift at the end of the year. Please write or e-mail for more details.